*Ian turned slightly toward her.
"So...you don't feel like drinking and
you don't feel like dancing. What do
you feel like doing?"*

Kissing you.

That thought popped into her head instantly, and she was glad that the words hadn't popped right out of her mouth. But it was the truth. She wanted to kiss Ian and be kissed by Ian. She wanted to be in his arms. She wanted the simple pleasure of holding his hand. She had given a pretty good speech the night before about being "just friends," but her heart wanted a much deeper connection with Ian than that. She wanted to ignore the flashing warning signs—bad timing or not, her heart was attaching itself to Ian.

Dear Reader,

Thank you for choosing *The One He's Been Looking For*! This love story is the second featuring the Brand family (Jordan had a cameo appearance in *A Baby for Christmas*). I chose San Diego and Curaçao as the backdrop for Jordan and Ian's romance because I'm crazy about both destinations. For a big city, San Diego has a really cool, laid-back vibe that I thought would be a great place for a romance. And I felt that the Dutch-owned Caribbean island Curaçao, with its historic beauty and pristine beaches, would be a wonderful place to fall in love. I had a blast living vicariously through Ian and Jordan as they discovered each other and fell in love in two of my favorite vacation spots. I hope that you enjoy reading *The One He's Been Looking For* as much as I enjoyed writing it. I always appreciate hearing from Harlequin readers, so please feel free to email me at jsimsromance@live.com. You can also follow me, @jsimsromance, on Facebook or Twitter. And be sure to stay tuned for more Brand Family romance....

All the best!

Joanna

The One He's Been Looking For

Joanna Sims

HARLEQUIN® SPECIAL EDITION®

Recycling programs
for this product may
not exist in your area.

ISBN-13: 978-0-373-65804-6

THE ONE HE'S BEEN LOOKING FOR

Printed in U.S.A.

Books by Joanna Sims

Harlequin Special Edition

A Baby For Christmas #2232
The One He's Been Looking For #2322

JOANNA SIMS

lives in Florida with her husband and their three fabulous felines. Joanna works as a therapist for the public school system during the day, but spends her evenings and weekends fulfilling her lifelong dream of writing compelling, modern romances for Harlequin. When it's time to take a break from writing, Joanna enjoys going for long walks with her husband and curling up on the couch to watch movies (romantic comedies preferably). She loves to answer any questions or provide additional information for her readers. You can contact her at joannasims2@live.com.

Dedicated to Martha:
Thank you for being a special part of my life.

Chapter One

Jordan Brand opened the throttle of her jet-black Ducati motorcycle and shot through the intersection just before the light turned red. She leaned forward as she aimed her bike between the two cars in front of her, determined to make up time by creating a third lane for herself. Jordan ignored the loud honking as she zipped in between the two lanes of traffic. She couldn't care less if the other drivers didn't like her shortcuts. This was California. *No one* had the right to cast stones.

Jordan cut off a canary-yellow Escalade as she made a right turn onto Broadway. She ignored the posted speed-limit sign. After all, sometimes tiny little rules needed to be broken. Jordan accelerated as she made another right onto Sixth and drove in the wrong direction up the one-way street. After dodging an oncoming car, she invented a parking spot in a no-parking zone and jammed on the brakes. She dropped the kickstand and shut off the engine.

"What lunatic actually thought it was a good idea to give you your license back?"

After she removed her helmet from her head, Jordan smiled broadly at the large, heavily tattooed man standing outside the tattoo parlor. "Which one of us has a better shot at makin' it to old age, Chappy? Me with my driving, or you with your cigarettes?"

Chappy grinned right before he took another drag from his unfiltered cigarette. "It's too close to call."

Jordan swung her leg over the seat of her bike, tucked her helmet under her arm and walked over to where he was standing. She reached up, pulled the cigarette out from between his lips, dropped it on the sidewalk and then crushed it beneath the heel of her boot.

"I just added a week to your life." She smiled up at him.

Chappy ran a beefy hand over his shaved, tattooed head. "If you come a little closer and give me a hug, I'll forgive you."

After she gave him a quick hug, Jordan asked, "Is Marty inside?"

"He's been waitin' on you, as usual. Got the client in the chair already. Don't you own a watch?"

Jordan stepped away from him with an easy laugh and pulled a rolled piece of paper from the inside pocket of her motorcycle jacket. "I have the drawing right here. When have I ever let you down?" She stopped just before she pulled open the door to the tattoo parlor. "You know, for social degenerates, the two of you are *really* uptight about punctuality."

"No." Ian Sterling slipped the top photo from the large stack of pictures in his hand and dropped it onto the floor.

"No," he said again, and the second photo followed the

first. He sifted quickly through the pile as he paced around his photography studio. "No. No. No. Dammit. No!"

Ian dropped the rest of the photographs onto the floor. He pulled off his reading glasses, marched over to his phone and stabbed at the intercom button with his finger. "Chelsea."

Dylan Axel, who was leaning casually against the desk, asked, "Is there a problem?"

Ian ignored him. "Chelsea. Come in here, please."

The door leading to the reception area opened and a tall, rail-thin brunette hurried in. "Yes, Mr. Sterling?"

Ian jerked his head toward the photographs strewn across the polished concrete floor. "Shred those."

Chelsea looked temporarily stunned but snapped out of it quickly. She lowered herself to the ground in her skintight pencil skirt and began to pick up the discarded pictures.

"I'm starting to think that you don't approve of the models I found." Dylan sauntered over to where Chelsea was teetering on her stiletto heels and offered his hand to her. "I'll take care of it, Chelsea. Thank you."

Chelsea's eyes shot to Ian before she allowed Dylan to help her to her feet.

"What I want," Ian said in frustration, "is just *one* model who doesn't have the same face that I've seen a million times before!"

Ian walked over to his receptionist. "Take Chelsea, for instance."

Dylan bent down and scooped up the head shots of the models he had found. He stood up and looked at his friend with apprehension. Usually he could count on Ian to be diplomatic, but lately, he'd become a loose cannon.

"She's a beautiful woman," Ian said to Dylan before he turned to Chelsea. "You're a beautiful woman."

"Thank you." Chelsea's smile brightened. Receiving a compliment from Ian Sterling was like winning the lottery for an aspiring model.

"But there's nothing new here, there's nothing *special* here. I'm looking for a face that I've haven't seen before, a face that makes me feel…*inspired*. Is that too much to ask?" Ian looked from one to the other of them questioningly.

His receptionist looked crestfallen and her smile faded. The color drained from her face as she spun on her heel and headed toward the door. She reached for the doorknob and slipped out. Dylan could hear the drawer of her desk being slammed shut. If she came back, he'd have to smooth things over with her.

"I don't know, Ian…." Dylan frowned at his long-time friend. "Is it too much to ask for you to be polite every once in a while?"

Ian glanced up, surprised to discover that Chelsea had left. He stared at the closed door for a second before he rubbed the back of his neck. He had been trying to make a point to Dylan, not insult Chelsea.

With a sigh, Ian said, "I'll talk to her when she gets back. I'll apologize."

"I know you well enough to know that you'll try to make it right, Ian. But here's a novel thought—let's get back to the days when you weren't regularly insulting folks. Let's bring that Ian back. I miss that guy."

Ian's jaw set. "I wouldn't waste my time thinking about that if I were you."

"Maybe you think it's a waste of time." Dylan dropped the head shots in an unceremonious pile on the desk. "But I don't."

When he didn't respond, Dylan continued. "Look. I get that you were handed a raw deal here, okay? Even when

I try to imagine what you're going through— Honestly, I can't. But let me ask you this—what good does it do you to take it out on everyone around you?"

"I said I'd apologize and I will," Ian said tersely. "But don't go holding your breath for the old Ian to come back, okay? He's dead."

Not waiting for his friend's answer, he walked over to the floor-to-ceiling windows that lined the walls of his studio, unlatched the plantation shutters that blocked out most of the natural light, and yanked them open. When the bright sunlight streamed into the room, he quickly covered his eyes with his hand. When he was twenty-eight, he had been diagnosed with a type of macular degeneration called Stargardt disease. Not only was the condition destroying his central vision, it had made his eyes sensitive to bright light.

"Dammit!" Ian grabbed his sunglasses from the inside pocket of his blazer and slipped them on quickly. The sunglasses worked double-duty—they had special lenses that helped him cope with light sensitivity, but also protected his eyes from UV rays that were destroying his central vision in the first place. Rain or shine, the sunglasses had become his constant companion.

Ian stood still for a moment, breathed in deeply until the pain in his eyes subsided. After a moment, he slowly, cautiously opened his eyes and looked down sullenly at the movement on the street below.

"Are you okay?" Dylan asked.

"I'm fine," he said roughly. It was a lie and they both knew it. But sometimes the lie was easier to handle.

Dylan shook his head. He felt powerless. No matter how hard he tried, he couldn't figure out how to help Ian and make things more…*tolerable.*

Ian continued to stare out at the city street below. He

hated the pity he heard in his friend's voice. Pity was the last thing he wanted. And that nerve-grinding sound of pity was exactly why he had worked so hard to keep his condition a secret. But keeping the secret was becoming increasingly difficult with each passing day. The truth was he had been living on borrowed time. Many people with Stargardt disease were legally blind by his age. He had been diagnosed later than most and the progression had been slow. The central vision in his left eye was completely blurred, but he still had his right eye. For now. But Ian couldn't ignore that changes were coming, just as he couldn't ignore that life as he knew it was about to drastically change.

The doctor who had unceremoniously broken the news to him that Stargardt was a "no treatment, no cure" one-way trip to legal blindness, had encouraged him to continue to exercise regularly, eat healthy, avoid foods rich in vitamin A and quit drinking alcohol ASAP. He'd referred him to a low-vision specialist and a psychologist to help him prepare for the changes to come. But how could anyone really prepare him to lose *everything* he loved: his career, his business…photography? Hadn't he *earned* the right to be angry?

"This book is part of my legacy as a photographer," Ian said in a controlled, quiet voice. His back was still turned to Dylan. "When all is said and done, and I can't see my own hand if I hold it up in front of my face, I'll know that this book exists. That my *work* lives on in it. That…*I* live on in it. Which means…I need a woman who can breathe life into every single shot. I need a woman who can help me make this book the *best* representation of Ian Sterling photography." He glanced over his shoulder at Dylan. "So excuse me if I feel a sense of urgency. We start shooting in a month and I haven't found her yet!"

Dylan jammed his hands into the front pockets of his tailored slacks. He understood why Ian was so driven to create a perfect book. He understood his focus, and even his foul mood. Ian felt he was on the brink of losing everything that he loved, and there wasn't anything he could do to stop it. No one could.

"What I need," Ian continued under his breath as he stared down onto the street below, "is a woman who's fearless, edgy, unique…someone with a personality. Not some California bleached-blond bimbo, or an Orphan Annie waif who needs a couple good meals. I want a woman who isn't afraid to be different. I want…" He paused for a moment as his eyes settled on a black motorcycle parked illegally and facing the wrong direction on Sixth Street. He could tell that the woman swinging her leg over the back of the bike was tall and lean. His heart began to quicken as he leaned forward and turned his head slightly to the left so he could focus in on her with his stronger eye. The minute she pulled off her helmet, he had a visceral response that felt like a punch in the gut.

"Her."

"What?" Dylan asked.

"Her," Ian repeated loudly. "Down there. I want *her.*"

"Mom. Mom! Will you come up for air, please? What's the problem?"

"I just saw the pictures on your Facebook page, Jordan! What have you done to your beautiful hair?"

"Cut it."

"I can *see* that. What did you do to the *color?*" Barbara Brand's voice had a shrill quality that made Jordan move the phone away from her ear for a minute.

"I changed it," she said nonchalantly when she brought the phone closer again.

"Jordan Carol, save your witticisms for your friends. Obviously I can *see* that you've changed the color from the pictures!"

"Mom." Jordan pushed on the door to leave the tattoo parlor; she smiled and winked at Chappy, who was tattooing a navy-themed design on a young man's arm. "If you're going to keep on freaking out every time I post a picture, I'm afraid we won't be able to be Facebook friends anymore."

Barbara ignored her daughter's teasing remark. "Your hair was so naturally beautiful, Jordan. Do you know how many women would pay good money to have hair like that? And look what you've gone and done. You've ruined it!"

"Mom. It's hair dye. It's not permanent."

"Not *permanent?*"

"Okay, let me rephrase that…it's not *forever.*"

"Your father thinks that it looks like a clown exploded on your head!"

"Uh…wow! I can't believe Dad said that! I'm not going to tell Amaya. She can be very sensitive about her work. It wasn't easy for her to get just the right blend of fire engine red, magenta madness and tangerine bliss."

"*Amaya?* Amaya did that? She isn't a hairstylist!"

"True," Jordan said of her roommate. "But she *is* a trained ice sculptor, among other things. We figured they were related disciplines." Jordan laughed as she stepped out onto the sidewalk.

After a short pause, Barbara added, "And here your dad went to all that trouble to get you an interview with the head of the art department at Montana State so you can finally finish your master's degree. What in the world are they going to think of you with that hair?"

Jordan stopped in her tracks and looked up at the sky in frustration. "Oh, my God, *Mom!* We've already discussed this like *a thousand times!* I am *not*...and I repeat...I am *not* moving to the middle of nowhere *Bozeman,* Montana. I'd rather die a slow and painful death!"

"What's wrong with Bozeman? It's a college town!" Barbara seemed genuinely surprised. "And you can paint anywhere after all. What's more inspiring than Montana in spring?"

"*Mom.* I have my first gallery show coming up. Do you know how insane it is that a gallery is actually willing to sponsor an unknown artist?" When her mother didn't respond, Jordan added, "Mom. I love you. But you've gotta accept that I'm not moving back to Montana."

Just as her mom was about to continue making her case, Jordan spotted a San Diego police officer standing beside her motorcycle. He was writing down her tag number.

"Hey! Wait!" she called out to the policeman. "Mom, I've gotta go. RoboCop is writing me a ticket."

"Jordan!"

She made a kissing sound into the phone. "I love you. Give Dad a hug for me!"

Jordan tapped the end call button and jammed her phone into her pocket. "Officer, wait. I'm gonna move it right now!"

The man had naturally golden skin, coal-black hair and the muscular frame of a guy who spent most of his spare time in the gym. He looked up at her and she saw that his eyes were the rich color of a Kona coffee bean. "Is this your motorcycle?"

"Yes."

"License, registration, proof of insurance." He was all business.

"Officer, please. I was just about to move it. I was late and—"

"License, registration, proof of insurance, ma'am." He was unmoved by her explanation, she could see.

Crap!

Jordan rested her helmet on the seat of her bike, pulled the license out of her back pocket and handed it to him.

The cop looked at the license and then said, "Registration, proof of insurance, Ms. Brand."

"I don't have it on me." Jordan inwardly cursed her own carelessness. How could she have left the house without her wallet?

"Wait here," the officer said before he walked back over to his own motorcycle.

Jordan followed him. "You don't understand. I just got my license back—"

"Stay with your vehicle, ma'am!" The cop stopped in his tracks and made a gesture that let her know he wasn't in the mood for any further argument or explanation.

Jordan took in a deep, frustrated breath as she walked back to her bike. She sat sidesaddle on the seat and stuffed her hands into the front pockets of her faded jeans.

As she watched the officer call her information in, all she could think of was the negative balance in her checking account. The money she'd just made selling customized tattoo designs to Marty needed to go into the account pronto if she had any hope of breaking even. It was a financial reality that occasionally selling tattoo designs and bartending on weekends at Altitude weren't enough to keep her right side up. But by her calculation, all she really needed to do was keep afloat until the gallery show. Then she'd be in the black. Well, that plan was looking like a real long shot now that RoboCop was about to blow up her flotation device.

Jordan was still calculating how screwed she was financially when her eyes were drawn to a man walking with long, determined strides in her direction. He was tall with a lean build, broad shouldered, and he walked with the natural swagger of a successful man who was wealthy *and* knew he was good-looking to boot. Just the type of man Jordan avoided like the plague: cocky, egoistical, narcissistic and way too *GQ* pretty for his own good.

"Wolf." The man spoke in a deep, authoritative baritone voice that was just as pleasant to the ears as his chiseled facial features were to the eyes. He didn't look her way as he stepped off the sidewalk and strode over to the officer. "Logan Wolf?"

The officer looked up from his notepad.

"I thought that was you." The well-dressed man didn't bother to take off his amber-colored sunglasses as he extended his hand. "Ian Sterling."

"Sterling Silver?" The policeman smiled and shook Ian's hand. "It took me a minute to recognize you. How the heck are you?"

"I'm good. Scouting a shoot."

"Around here? I've seen you on TV a couple times and I thought, 'not bad for a guy the senior class voted as most likely to get arrested.'"

Ian smiled briefly. "If I remember correctly, you tied me for that honor."

Officer Wolf laughed. "I was hoping you'd forgotten about that, in light of my current profession."

Jordan listened to the exchange between the two men with growing impatience. She was tired, hungry and she wished that GQ and RoboCop would have their little frat-boy reunion on someone else's time.

"Listen, I'm sorry if I made you get out your pad for nothing," Ian said.

"What do you mean?"

She was just about to interrupt their little reunion party

when Ian gestured to her. "She's one of my models. I asked her to park here, and she shouldn't get a ticket for something I asked her to do."

"You asked her?" The cop sounded skeptical as he glanced over at her.

"That's right," Ian said smoothly as he tried, unsuccessfully, to read the name on her license. "And I'd really appreciate it if we could just call this a warning."

RoboCop didn't look totally convinced as he tapped his pen on the ticket pad. For whatever reason, this Ian character was attempting to help her beat the ticket, and she fully intended to do her part in order for him to succeed.

Jordan pushed away from the motorcycle, walked straight over to Ian and said, "You're late, Mr. Sterling."

GQ looked down at her and examined her from behind his sunglasses, just as if he was examining a bug trapped in a glass jar.

"I'm sorry about that. A conference call held me up," he said. Jordan had the distinct feeling that giving an apology, even a *fake* apology, left a bitter taste in this man's mouth.

Finally, after what seemed to be an eternity, Officer Wolf released her license from his clipboard and extended it to her. "I'm going to let you off with a warning this time, Ms. Brand."

Jordan let out her breath, which she hadn't even realized she was holding in, and plucked the license from his gloved fingers.

"Thank you, Officer." She slipped the license into her back pocket.

"Thanks, Wolf. I owe you one."

Logan Wolf gave a slight shake of his head as he sat down on his motorcycle. "You bet, Sterling. Just make sure she moves the bike ASAP."

"Will do." Ian reached into his wallet and pulled out a

business card. "It was good seeing you again. Let's catch up sometime."

Logan took the card and tucked it into the front pocket of his uniform. "Sounds good."

The minute the officer drove away, Jordan turned on her heel and headed back to her bike.

GQ followed her. "My name is Ian Sterling."

Jordan picked up her helmet and slipped it on. "So I've heard."

Ian held out a business card to her. She didn't take it. Instead, she swung her leg over the motorcycle seat and sat down.

"I'm a photographer," he added.

She pushed the motorcycle upright. "Congratulations."

She couldn't see his eyes, but she read the slight tightening around his sculpted mouth as displeasure with her response. No doubt he was used to getting his way with women *all* the time.

"I want to photograph you."

Jordan gave a sharp laugh as she slipped the key into the ignition. "Uh...*wow!* That was a genuinely pathetic pickup line."

"I'm not trying to pick you up. I'm a photographer." Irritation had crept into his tone. He pointed to the old Lion Clothing building that had been converted to lofts. "My studio's right up there."

"Listen, mister, just because you helped me out with RoboCop doesn't mean I owe you a massage with a happy ending. Got it?"

Before Ian could reply, the brass bell attached to the tattoo parlor door clanged loudly as Chappy shoved the door open. "This joker bothering you, Jordan?"

Most people had the good sense to be intimated by the

burly biker. Ian, Jordan noticed, remained unimpressed, and didn't take a step back from her.

"No." She started her bike. "I was just leaving." She revved her engine for a second before she shifted into gear. "A parting word of advice, GQ. Get some new material."

Jordan slid the visor of her helmet into place and pulled out onto Sixth Street. Ian watched her as she disappeared up the road; no question about it, he wanted her for the book. From her striking cheekbones to her a lovely heart-shaped face and those shocking cat-shaped blue eyes, Jordan was perfect. The interesting angles of her features and her "in-your-face" attitude made her...*fascinating.* He knew instinctively that she was the one he'd been searching for. She had everything he wanted: energy, intensity, beauty.

"You got some sorta problem, Jack?" Chappy glared at him.

Ian slipped his business card back into his wallet. "None that are any of your business, *Jack.*"

As he headed back to his studio, his thoughts were fixated on the beautiful woman on the Ducati. And thanks to Wolf and the biker, he knew her first name *and* her last name. Now all he had to do was track her down.

Chapter Two

Jordan stepped out onto the narrow foyer of her condo and pulled the door shut. The early-September ocean breeze blowing in from the harbor brushed across her skin as she stepped out onto the curb. There was a chill in the air that made her glad that she had chosen her skinny jeans and ankle boots over her favorite microminiskirt. Jordan crossed Island Avenue and headed toward the trolley station. As she walked along First Avenue, a black Bentley parked in the lot directly across from her condo caught her attention. She watched as the chauffeur got out, hurried around the front of the vehicle and opened the door for the passenger to exit. It was an odd place for the Bentley to be parked. As Jordan walked directly in front of it, the passenger stepped out from behind the chauffeur. She recognized him instantly.

Ian Sterling!

Shocked, Jordan stumbled on a break in the sidewalk.

She paused temporarily before she started to walk at a hurried pace toward the trolley. This wasn't a coincidence. GQ was actually *stalking* her! Jordan quickened her steps as she reached in her pocket; her fingers wrapped around a small, pink, lipstick-size container of mace. He might be bigger than her, but she wasn't about to go down easily *or* quietly.

"Jordan!"

She heard the leather soles of Ian's shoes slap the cement as he pursued her. Jordan lengthened her stride, but wasn't naive enough to believe that she could outwalk him.

"Jordan!"

Irritated and unnerved, she stopped in her tracks and spun around. *"What?"* she asked in a shaky voice. "What do you *want?* Why are you following me?" She pulled out her phone and prepared to hit speed dial for 911.

In three long strides, Ian was in front of her. "I've got business to discuss with you."

Jordan shook her head in disbelief. "How did you find me? Do you have *any idea* how frickin' nuts this is?" She continued to shake her head. "You know what? Forget it! I'm calling the cops *right now* unless you get lost pronto, buddy. And if I so much as see you anywhere near my house again, I'll file a restraining order against you so fast your pretty-boy head will spin! Are we clear?"

Ian held up his hands in surrender. "I'm not trying to hurt you, Jordan. I'm trying to hire you."

"Did I *ask* you for a job?" she snapped. "No. I don't think I did! But what I am asking is for you to *leave me alone.* Am I speaking in tongues? Why are we having a failure to communicate?"

Jordan spun around and began to walk with purposeful strides away from Ian. She glanced over her shoulder once and was grateful that he hadn't moved from his spot.

"Jordan," he called after her. "Five minutes. That's all I'm asking." He paused, and then added, "Please."

There was a raw sincerity in his tone that made her halt in her tracks; she slowly turned back to him. The sun was waning, but the man still had his sunglasses on. She could barely see his eyes behind the dark amber lenses.

"What do you want, GQ? Really. What do you *really* want from me?"

Ian took one small step forward. "Like I said the first time we met…I want to photograph you."

"And why, might I ask, would the great Ian Sterling want to photograph me?"

Her question made him pause for a split second before he stated, "You know who I am."

Jordan narrowed her eyes, angry that she had let it slip out inadvertently that she had looked him up on the internet. She was caught red-handed, so there was no sense denying it.

"I did a Google search. Ian Sterling…" She waved her hand in front of her body as if she was drawing a large rainbow. "Photographer to the stars. Yes. I know who you are, and the question still remains, why would someone like *you* want to photograph someone like *me?*"

Ian took another step toward her and answered her question seriously. "You have the face I've been looking for."

Jordan kept her hand wrapped tightly around the small bottle of mace in her pocket while she thought about his words. She just couldn't figure out his angle. He seemed sincere, but that didn't mean that he *was*. She hadn't spent much time researching him, but from what she had read, Ian was internationally known and highly respected.

He took another small step forward. "Listen…all I want to do is test you for my next book. I promise you—the offer's legit."

Before Jordan had a chance to reply, her phone rang. She slipped her hand off the mace and pulled the phone out of her pocket.

"Hey," she said as she kept her eyes trained on Ian. "I'm just about to hop on the trolley. I'll be there in a sec."

She clicked off the phone and said, "Listen. I've gotta go."

"What about my job offer?"

Jordan paused for a moment and then shrugged one shoulder. "I'm not a model, Mr. Sterling. You've got the wrong woman."

"If you test well, I'll pay you twenty-five thousand dollars for your time."

Once again, Jordan stopped in her tracks. She slowly pirouetted until she was facing him again. "What did you say?"

This time, he stayed rooted in place. She could see that he was done chasing her for the moment. "You heard me. Five thousand up front. Twenty when we're done shooting. Plus expenses."

"Please." Her arched brows drew together. "You can't be serious."

"Try me."

Jordan tilted her head slightly to the side. "Are you willing to put that in writing?"

"I wouldn't have it any other way."

She chewed on her lower lip and narrowed her eyes as she mulled over the offer. Twenty-five thousand dollars could buy a heck of a lot of canvas and paint. She'd be *swimming* in art supplies, not to mention that her rent would be paid for months in advance. Her money worries would be over, at least temporarily, and she could concentrate full-time on the paintings for her first gallery showing. And for what? Posing for a couple pictures? Smiling pretty for the camera? She'd be a fool to say no. And yet...

Ian interrupted her train of thought. "My car's right over there. If you're late, I can take you anywhere you need to go. We can talk on the way."

Jordan shook her head at him disbelievingly. "Just because I haven't maced you yet doesn't mean I'm crazy enough to get into a car with a complete stranger and be taken God knows where! It still hasn't been determined that you *aren't* a very nicely dressed serial killer."

"You yourself said that you know who I am."

"Please." Jordan laughed. "Just because you're famous doesn't mean that you're not a total freak. In fact, being famous is a huge strike against you, in my opinion."

"Is that a 'no' to my offer?"

Jordan turned and headed toward the station. "That's an 'I don't know.'"

Ian waved his hand at the driver before he caught up with Jordan.

"I have to catch this trolley. I'll think about it." She quickened her pace as the A trolley pulled in.

Ian stayed with her and, as the doors to the vehicle opened, followed her to her seat and sat down on the bench across from her. He spread out his long legs in front of him and draped one arm over the back of his seat. Jordan would have thought he would look out of place sitting there in his dark gray pin-striped suit and his deep purple shirt, but surprisingly, he looked just as relaxed and in charge on the trolley as he did standing next to his Bentley.

"Ride the trolley often, do you?" Jordan asked drily.

"Never," he admitted easily. He was so ridiculously handsome, so well made, that it was hard for her to stop staring at his face. She wasn't certain she had ever met anyone quite as perfectly good-looking as Ian Sterling. Of course, he was totally not her type. She was chronically attracted to scruffy musicians and moody out-of-work artists. It was a bit of sickness, really. Lately she had been thinking that it was time to change her brand of men.

"What's up with the sunglasses anyway? Are you going for Michael Jackson circa 1982?"

"I'm sensitive to light," he answered smoothly. It was the truth and made it easy to explain why he wore sunglasses even on cloudy days or at dusk. Most people accepted it or just didn't care.

"Okay." Jordan scoffed sarcastically. "Sure."

She saw Ian work his jaw before he reached up and pulled off his sunglasses. He narrowed his eyes against the light and looked at her. Although the vision in his left eye was fuzzy and blurred, he was able to see Jordan's face with his right eye. Focusing on what he could see with his right while ignoring his left was a skill he had mastered early on in the diagnosis. To look at him directly, no one would suspect he was slowly losing his ability to see.

For the first time, Jordan was able to see Ian's intense blue-gray eyes as he stared back at her. A jolt of instant recognition coursed through her system as she locked gazes with Ian. There was something so *familiar* about this man. She just couldn't put her finger on it. As the trolley pulled away from the station, she drew out her phone and held it up to his face. She pressed a button.

Ian frowned at her. "Did you just take my picture?"

"Yes." Jordan dropped her head as she punched more buttons on the device.

"Why?" His voice sharpened on the question.

Jordan was certain he was used to getting his way very quickly when he used that tone. She ignored him and finished her chore before she answered. "What? Oh, I'm *sorry*. Did that bother you? Was that an invasion of your *privacy?* I mean, *God forbid* that should happen to you, a famous photographer. I mean, what's the big deal? I just took a picture, it's not like I tracked you down at your *private residence* or followed you onto a trolley...."

Ian didn't respond, but she could see by the stony expression on his face that she had made her point.

"I just sent your picture to all of my friends. If anything happens to me, the police will come knocking on your door first," Jordan said smugly. Then she leaned back on her bench and stared at him curiously. "How'd you find me anyway?"

He dragged his fingers over his closely cropped brown hair. "I know someone who's good at finding people."

She looked out at the darkening downtown skyline and muttered, "Privacy is obsolete." Jordan glanced quickly at his strong, masculine profile. Her gut was telling her that Ian wasn't a psycho and he wasn't out for anything other than a photograph. In fact, she suspected that he didn't see her as a woman in the sexual-object sense of the word; his examination of her was much too...clinical for that. He wasn't really looking at *her,* but seemed to be taking an inventory of her features.

"Were you serious about the money?" she asked in a lowered voice.

Ian didn't hesitate. "Yes."

Jordan leaned forward and rested her elbows on her knees. The bangles on her arm slipped forward and jangled on their journey down to her wrist. "But why? Why would you give some woman you spotted on the street that much money?"

"Some of the best models have been discovered exactly that way." He paused for a split second and then added, "And it's not all that much money."

"Maybe not to you." Jordan wrinkled her brow. "Either way, I'm no Gisele Bündchen."

"I wouldn't want you to be," Ian replied. "But interestingly, Gisele *was* discovered in a McDonalds by scouts, so…"

Jordan knew that he had wanted to make a point with that comment, and the truth was he succeeded. It wasn't a secret that many famous models were discovered on the street or at a mall. She hadn't known that about Gisele, but it didn't really surprise her. In fact, this wasn't the first time she had been approached. She was five foot ten by the time she was fourteen, so she had been asked to model before. The problem was that she wasn't what one might call photogenic. And even though the money was extremely tempting, Jordan was convinced that she couldn't pull it off. She simply photographed badly. Always had. Every single one of her school pictures was hideous and she had always been the one blaring *flaw* in the yearly Brand family portraits.

"Listen, I appreciate the offer, and I'd be lying if I didn't say that the money sounds good, but I can't model for you." Jordan watched the muscle in Ian's jaw clench as he listened to her. He was completely unaccustomed to the sound of the word *no.* "And even though I think that it was totally out of line for you to *stalk* me, I'm still sorry you wasted your time."

"I'm a little confused about why you won't even agree to test for me. Is it the money?"

"As in, not *enough* money?"

Ian gave a slight nod; Jordan laughed. "No, it's not the money. Trust me—the money'd be *great* right now."

She had the distinct feeling that if she had said it *wasn't* enough money, he would have immediately offered her more.

"Then what?" Ian appreciated the way Jordan's eyes crinkled at the corners when she laughed. She laughed as if she really meant it.

Jordan sat back and crossed one leg over the other. "Look. I'm going to be honest with you so we can drop this subject for good and you can go find a different model for your book."

"All right."

"I'm not photogenic," she said simply.

"I don't believe that."

"I'm telling you the truth. Whether or not you believe it is your business. You're not the first person who's tried to turn me into a model. But for whatever reason—" Jordan waved her hand in front of her face "—this doesn't look the same in a photograph as it does in person."

As the trolley pulled into the next station, Jordan stood up. She extended her hand. "Well…it's been interesting."

Ian stood, as well. Jordan hoped that he didn't intend to follow her off the tram.

Instead of taking her hand, he slipped a business card into her fingers. "When *I* photograph you, you'll be able to see yourself as I see you. Pure avant-garde beauty."

Her heart gave a quick, hard thump at his words. This man had a way of twisting a woman right around his well-manicured pinky.

Jordan took the card. "If you can make me look good in a picture, you would be the first."

"Come to my studio tomorrow and let's find out," he said.

"What do I have to lose?" she asked out loud, more to herself than to him.

"Twenty-five thousand dollars."

The trolley doors slid open. "Touché, Mr. Sterling."

"Ian."

Jordan stepped down onto the curb. "Touché, *Ian*."

"You'll come to my studio, then."

She turned to face him as he stood in the doorway, hands in his pockets, sunglasses back in place. Tall, broad shouldered and built for a woman's appreciating eye. He appeared to be perfectly at ease on the surface, but Jordan picked up a tension in his jaw that belied his relaxed, confident stance.

"What time?"

"Eight in the morning."

"Too early."

"Ten, then."

As the trolley door began to slide shut, Jordan flashed Ian a peace sign and said, "I'll be there around eleven."

"Rise and shine, lazybones."

The next morning, Jordan was rudely awakened by the sound of her twin sister's "cheerful early riser" voice. She groaned and stuck her head under the pillow as Josephine pulled open the blinds and let sunlight flow into the room. Jordan squeezed her eyes shut as she tried to ignore the sound of the thick plastic blinds slapping against each other as they settled back into place.

Josephine plopped down on the bed next to her and began to shake her shoulder. "Wake up. Wake up. Wake up...."

"Oh, my God, Jo!" Jordan grumbled loudly. "Knock it off!"

"Not a chance." Her sister laughed as she grabbed the pillow and pulled it off her head.

Jordan made a frustrated noise as she dragged the covers over her head. She hadn't planned on being awake for at least another hour or two. "Go away!"

Next, Jo started to bounce up and down. "Get up. Get up. Get up!"

Jordan finally kicked the blanket and sheets off her body and glared up at her. "Holy crap, Jo, you're annoying! What are you doing here? Aren't you supposed to be learning how to sue people?"

Josephine, whose friends and family called her "Jo," was her identical twin. They were mirror images of each other in appearance, but exact opposites in life. Jo was an "early bird gets the worm" student working on her law degree, while Jordan had dropped out of graduate school five weeks into her masters. Jo loved to shop, was a political junky, recycled religiously and thought that it was perfectly normal to date a young environmental lawyer named *Brice*. Besides the recycling, Jordan could live without all those things—especially a boyfriend with a country-club name.

Jo smiled at her sister's trademark early-morning grouchiness. "I'm meeting Brice and his parents for brunch in Van Nuys. I thought I'd drop by for a quick visit."

Jordan pushed herself up and leaned back against the headboard. "I find you to be rude and offensive on all possible levels."

"You love me." Jo smiled broadly.

Jordan squinted at her sister through sore, puffy eyes, wishing she had the motivation to get up and shut the blinds again. The bright sunlight was only making her pounding hangover headache worse. To look at the two of them, someone would be hard-pressed to make out that they were twins at all. Josephine always looked like the healthy girl next door with her flowing, sun-kissed hair and glowing, sun-kissed skin. Jordan, on the other hand, was a rebellious night-owl artist with a multicolored faux hawk and pale skin that barely saw the sunlight. In a lot of ways, they were truly night and day.

"How you can date someone named *Brice* is beyond me," Jordan said as she rubbed the sleep out of her eyes. "Much less have brunch with his parents."

"Quit being such a snob. He didn't choose his name," Jo teased. "By the way, you look hungover."

"That's because I *am* hungover, Nancy Drew." Jordan squinted at her. "Joelle had a pink-champagne fountain at her bachelorette party. Who *does* that?"

"You could've said no." Jo went into the bathroom; she grabbed a glass of water and two aspirin. "Here."

"Thanks." Jordan popped the pills in her mouth and then chugged down the water.

"I thought you liked Brice anyway." Her twin perched on the edge of the bed again in her pretty forest-green wrap dress.

"I like him in theory." Jordan put the empty glass on the nightstand.

"Whatever that's supposed to mean…."

"It means that he *seems* like someone who'd be perfect for you, but he's not because he's actually a total knuckle-dragger."

Jo raised her perfectly shaped eyebrows at her before saying, "Subject change."

"Agreed."

Jo pulled her phone out of her purse, flipped through her text messages and then held up a picture for Jordan to see. "I'm dying to know… How'd you end up with a picture of the Armani guy on your phone?"

Jordan stared at the picture she had taken on the trolley. He looked handsome, of course, and ticked off. "That's Ian. He's a photographer."

Jo looked at the image with a shake of her head. "Well,

then, he must have been a model before he was a photographer, because I'm telling you, that's the Armani guy. How you could have your fantasy man sitting *right in front of you* and not recognize him is a total brainteaser."

"I didn't recognize him because it *isn't* him," Jordan said as she climbed out of bed. She pulled on a pair of jeans that had been crumpled up on the floor. "I need emergency coffee."

The twins climbed up the narrow spiral staircase to the second-floor kitchen and dining area. Amaya was sitting at the small dining table eating sushi with finely carved black-and-gold chopsticks.

"Coffee?" Jordan asked her roommate at the top of the stairs.

Amaya nodded and pointed to the kitchen. Jordan grabbed a cup of coffee for herself and one for Jo before she headed to the table.

"What time did you get in?" Amaya asked in her Cambodian-accented English. She had twisted her silky blue-black hair into a thick topknot at the crown of her head and she still had a smudge of purple eye shadow above her dark chocolate eyes from the night before.

Jordan slumped into her chair and gratefully took a sip of piping-hot coffee. "Three, four. I'm not sure, really."

Her roommate swallowed a bite of food before she said, "What's up with that picture you sent to me last night? Who is that guy?"

Jordan dropped her head onto her arms with a groan. "He's a photographer. Wants me to model for him."

Jo's eyes widened. "The Armani guy wants you to *model* for him? You didn't tell me that!"

"*Jesus*...he's not the Armani guy. His name is Ian Sterling."

"Seriously, Jordy? I can't believe you didn't recognize

him." Her twin shook her head as she searched for something on her phone. Once she found what she was looking for, she held up the device triumphantly. "Take a look at this, sis. Tell me that isn't the same guy."

Chapter Three

Jordan's forehead wrinkled as she stared at the photograph on Jo's phone. It took a split second for her to recognize Ian in the Armani ad. His hair was longer and his face thinner, but there was no doubt it was Ian. No wonder he looked so familiar to her! She had this exact ad hanging up in her room…framed. How had she *missed* that?

"Ho-ly crap." she muttered. "He's the frickin' Armani guy."

"Told you," Jo said smugly.

"What am I missing?" Amaya asked.

"Jordan had this ad hanging above her bed when we were in high school—she used to kiss the guy's picture every night. Swore she was going to marry him," Jo said, before she blew on her coffee.

"Do you think that might have been an overshare of my personal information?" Jordan asked her sister.

Jo ignored her and continued, "As it turns out…" She

turned the phone toward Amaya. "This guy and the guy from last night are one and the same."

"Freaky." Amaya studied the picture. "He's seriously hot."

"Yes," Jordan agreed, as her high school fantasies flooded her brain. "He is.

"Does he really look that good in person or was he edited to look like that?" Amaya asked before she took another bite of her sushi.

Jordan shook her head. Ian Sterling didn't need to be edited. He was damn near perfect. "No. He really does look like this."

She groaned as she dropped her head into her hands and rubbed her temples. How could she have missed this when she'd found him on Google? How could she have missed it when she'd sat across from him on the trolley? And now she was supposed to go to his studio—the Armani guy's studio—looking as if she had been on a week-long bender? *Unimaginable.*

"Start from the beginning—tell us everything," Jo said, her blue eyes sparkling.

Jordan lifted her head and took a deep breath in through her nose and then blew it out. She told them everything—from Ian saving her from a ticket to him tracking her down at the condo and offering her a job.

She finished her story with, "I'm supposed to go to his studio today for a test shoot."

Jo smiled at her as she reached out and shook her arm. "It's serendipitous! You always make fun of me when I tell you stuff like this happens. But come *on*.... What are the chances?"

"Slim to none," Jordan admitted as she stared at the Armani ad.

Amaya asked bluntly, "And you're sure he's not a wacko

who's gonna chop you up and stuff you in his freezer, right?"

"I'm pretty sure he's not a psycho." Jordan said.

"Then this is *great* news. You're saved! Rent's due in a week and I can't cover the spread for both of us again this month."

"Why did she have to pay your rent last month?" Jo asked, concerned.

"It's not a big deal." Jordan brushed off the question before she responded to Amaya. "I don't think I can do it. I feel like death warmed over and…"

Amaya gave her an incredulous look. "Let me get this straight. You've got a hot photographer wanting to pay you to take your picture, and you don't know? Are you *nuts?* You've gotta pull it together, Jordy, and go make bank. If you don't, you're gonna have to take up panhandling, or even worse, go crawling back to your family. You don't want that, do you?"

"God, no!" Jordan knew her roommate was right. She was almost broke and the last thing she wanted to do was run back to her parents for money, not with her mom's one-woman campaign to get her to move back to Montana.

Jo continued to stare her down as Amaya took her plate to the kitchen. "What?" Jordan asked defensively.

"Why didn't you make rent, Jordy? What happened to the money you get from Grandpa's trust?"

"That stopped once I dropped out of graduate school. I won't get the balance until I'm thirty." She shook her head.

"And you couldn't ask Mom and Dad? I know they'd help out."

Jordan sighed in frustration. "Of course they would. But there's always strings attached with Mom, and you know it. And for some reason, ever since…Daniel, she's fixated on the idea of me moving back to Montana. She already has Tyler at the ranch with her—why is she hell-bent on having me there, too?"

"You're the baby."

"By ten minutes!" Jordan exclaimed. Her mother had had five children. Luke, the eldest son, had had an identical twin named Daniel, who had died in the Iraq war. Tyler, the middle child, was being groomed to take over Bent Tree, the family ranch, once their father retired. And then there was Josephine, and finally herself—the baby of the family.

"You know she only wants what's best for you," Jo said as she finished her coffee.

"I know." Jordy agreed easily. "But she's driving me crazy—and this time she's just flat-out wrong."

"Well, sis, if you're gonna keep a roof over your head or have the occasional meal, it looks like your best bet is to take Mr. Armani Ad up on his offer."

Jordan stared at her twin for several seconds and let her words sink in. She couldn't deny that her levelheaded sister had a point.

"Crap." Jordan finally dropped her head into her hands yet again. She had no doubt this was going to shape up to be a horrifying day.

Jordan arrived at the Samuel Fox Lofts at 12:30 p.m. She made certain that she parked legally before heading up to the third floor. She pulled Ian's business card from the back pocket of her skintight black jeans and looked for the apartment number. At the end of the hall, she found the loft door adorned with a small plaque that read Sterling & Axel Photography.

Jordan opened the door and stepped into a small reception area decorated with high-fashion photographs featuring models and actresses alike. There wasn't a receptionist sitting at the desk, so she walked over to the next door and opened it slowly. She poked her head in and was greeted by a long, narrow room with high ceilings. The floor-to-ceiling windows were covered with closed plantation shutters, the concrete floors were stained and polished, and exposed-brick structural columns separated the open space into two halves. Just to the left of the door was a large sitting area with a modern, black leather, U-shaped couch. Two leggy females, models, presumably, were sprawled out on it. Both couch loungers inspected her with unsmiling, sullen faces.

"Are you Jordan?"

She was startled by the sound of another female's voice. Jordan swiveled her head and looked down at a petite, curvy Latina who had just walked up behind her carrying a cup of coffee.

Jordan had to step into the loft in order to make room for the woman. "Yes."

"I'm Violet Rios, Ian's makeup artist." She brushed past Jordan and then stopped. "*Dios mío,* you're late! I didn't think you were gonna show, and Ian's pissed. Close the door and come with me. I doubt that he's gonna want to shoot you today. If a model's late, he *never* uses them."

Jordan followed her into the loft, thinking she wouldn't mind a bit if he changed his mind about photographing her. Her head was pounding and she had an acrid taste in her mouth that no amount of gargling had been able to combat. The sound of the rapid-fire clicking of Violet's heels on the concrete floor bounced off the high ceilings and only intensified her headache. Those multiple glasses of pink champagne were hanging on for dear life. What a mistake!

Violet led her to a small room near the kitchen. "Wait in here."

The woman took a quick sip of her coffee before she

put the cup down on her makeup table, dropped her large red hobo bag on the floor and disappeared.

Jordan sighed heavily as she slouched into the director's chair, which faced a brightly illuminated oval mirror, and stared at her reflection. Her coloring was sallow, her eyes were bloodshot and there was no mistaking that she was hungover. She dropped her head into her hands and rubbed her temples. She could only pray that Ian was so fed up with her that he booted her out of his studio. Of course, that would leave her without her share of the rent for the month. It was a lose-lose situation.

She didn't lift her head up when she heard the annoying clack of Violet's heels and the deep, silky baritone of Ian's voice just outside the door. Like a child, she was hoping that if she couldn't see them, they couldn't see her.

"You're late." She could feel the heat of the photographer's body on her arm. She breathed in and caught the spicy scent that could only be coming from his warm, tan skin.

Slowly she lifted her head and squinted at him through narrowed, bloodshot eyes. Instead of apologizing, which she knew she should do, because that was what she was *raised* to do, she defaulted to sarcasm. He made her nervous, and when she was nervous, the sarcasm flowed unchecked.

"Would you mind keeping it down? My head is *killing* me."

"I'll bet." Ian didn't bother to hide his annoyance.

He was standing directly in front of her, arms crossed over his defined chest. He was dressed more casually today in a fitted T-shirt and jeans, which only seemed to add to his appeal. Her heart picked up its pace when she looked up into his face. How could a real live human actually be that good-looking? Yes, the angles of his face were more defined, his hair was cut close to his scalp and there were lines etched in his forehead and around his eyes that hadn't been there before. But there was no mistaking that Ian *was* the man she'd had hanging on her wall in high school. The man she'd fantasized about for years. He unnerved her now, and she couldn't remember the last time anyone had made her feel that way.

His eyes swept her face in that clinical manner of his. He knew she was hungover; she waited for him to say the magic words: *get lost.* But they never came. She didn't know whether to be relieved or horrified.

Instead of giving her the boot, Ian ignored her and addressed Violet, who was standing to his left with the corners of her glossy, full lips pressed down into a frown. "Give her a nude mouth, emphasize the eyes, but don't overdo it.... I want her to look fresh. Natural. And for God's sake, try to do something with the dark circles and the bloodshot eyes. She looks like she's been up for a week."

"What about the hair?"

Jordan didn't appreciate them speaking over her head as if she was an oversize stuffed doll they were dressing up.

"Twist it back off her face. I don't want anything to detract from her face. Keep the jeans, but lose the combat boots and the T-shirt. Put her in a white tank." Ian turned to her and asked, "Do you have on a bra?"

"Excuse me?" Was the Armani guy from her high school wet dreams asking her about foundation garments?

"Do you have on a bra?"

Jordan glanced down at her barely there bust and shook her head. "Lifting and separating has never been a concern."

"Get her a bra if she wants one. And have her fill out the release form before you bring her in." Ian said to Violet before he exited the room without glancing Jordan's way again.

Violet worked quickly and silently, and within in a short time Jordan had been transformed, much to her surprise, into a woman who actually resembled a model. She leaned forward and examined her reflection.

"That's *cra-zy*," she exclaimed. "How'd you do that?"

Even to her own critical eye, she looked like a solid eight on a ten-point scale.

Violet ignored her question and held out her hands for the filled-out release forms. "Come on," she said in her bored, bossy tone. "He's waited long enough for you today."

Jordan followed her to the back of the studio, to a small area surrounded by reflectors and tall, bright lights. Ian was setting up one of his cameras.

"She's all yours," Violet said before she turned on her heel and headed back to her room.

Ian spun around and strode over to where Jordan was standing; he examined her hair and makeup. She stood perfectly still and held her breath for some ridiculous reason. Why should she care if he approved? But she did.

His eyes finally stopped and locked onto hers. "You clean up well."

Typically, she would have a snappy comeback, but at the moment her mind was a blank. She felt as if her legs had turned to cement, and she was feeling a bit nauseous again. She was completely out of her element.

This wasn't a seedy, dark artist's dungeon filled with disenfranchised, unemployed kindred spirits. This was frickin' ridiculously handsome Armani-model photographer-to-the-stars *Ian Sterling's* studio. She didn't fit in here. What had she been thinking?

"Blink if you can hear me," Ian said in a lowered voice that was meant for her ears only.

"I don't know what I'm doing here." The honesty bubbled out unchecked. She must be more freaked out than she'd thought.

He reached out and placed his palms on her bare shoulders. His large, warm hands engulfed them as he moved his mouth closer to her ear. "You're here for the money."

The sensation of his breath on her skin released a swarm of butterflies in her stomach. She nodded her head slightly and tightened her abdominal muscles in an attempt to get the stupid things under control. This was the wrong time to get all stirred up. She needed to focus on what the man was saying, not the sensation his breath was creating as he was saying it.

Focus, Jordy! Focus!

After a moment, she was able to refocus her brain on Ian's words. The man had made perfect sense and his point was undeniably valid. She *was* here for the money. She didn't understand why she was being such a chicken, but the thought of not being able to make rent snapped her out of it. With a renewed sense of purpose, she squared her shoulders, rolled them out from underneath Ian's hands and elevated her chin.

"What now?" she asked.

"Now? You pose, I shoot. Simple." He walked over to a table and reached for one of the cameras placed there. "Are you ready?"

"Sure." She said it with a bravado she didn't really feel.

The minute Ian picked up the camera, she saw him transform. He had the same look on his face that she imagined she had on hers when she set up a brand-new canvas and opened up a fresh tube of paint. Holding the camera in his hand seemed to electrify him. It was strange, but this was first time he'd actually seemed truly *alive*. The man obviously loved his job.

"I want to be flexible today, but I definitely want to get a beauty shot of you. Do you know what that is?"

"I've watched modeling shows on television before."

Ian smiled at her. "So you're practically a pro."

For the next several seconds all she could do was stare mindlessly at his perfectly straight, perfectly formed white teeth.

"Those have to be veneers." She heard herself speaking her thoughts aloud like a freak. Was she still drunk? Had she developed sudden-onset Tourette's? What was she *talking* about?

"What?" he asked.

"What?" She answered his question with a question, and pretended that she hadn't said a word. She forced herself to drag her eyes away from his mouth.

For an awkward minute, they looked at each other curiously before Ian moved on from her odd comment and explained, "A beauty shot simply means that I'll be focusing on your face. But don't let your body get stiff—relax and move."

"Relax and move," Jordan repeated.

"And the most important thing for you to remember is to keep the intensity in your eyes," Ian continued. "The eyes sell the shot…which is why a beauty shot can be one of the hardest for a model to master."

"Shouldn't you let me ride with the training wheels on first?" she asked. They had drawn a crowd. Everyone in the loft, including the two famished models from the couch, were standing at the edge of the set.

Ian gestured for her to move over until she was standing in front of a large white screen. "You ride a Ducati, so you don't need training wheels," he said as he aimed his camera at her.

Standing in front of Ian now, Jordan felt completely vulnerable and exposed in the filmy white tank top. She made a good show of being a rebel with a cause, but underneath it all, she was just a conservative girl from Montana.

"Okay." He seemed oblivious to her discomfort. "Let's get started."

He took a couple more shots to test the lighting. He checked the computer monitor and then nodded. "Lighting's good.... Now focus on me, Jordan. Forget everything else." The gravelly quality of his voice as he said her name sent a shiver racing right up her spine.

Jordan breathed in deeply and tried to put the audience out of her mind, but she could see the praying mantis twins burning holes into her flesh from the corner of her eye. Another flash popped.

"Look straight into the camera. Chin up just a little bit. Relax your mouth. Good, Jordan. Very nice."

She tried to relax, but instead just felt stupid and awkward.

"Look at me *through* the lens. Nice. I like it, Jordan. Hold that, please."

The flashbulb popping drew her attention back to Ian again and again. But no matter how hard she tried to follow his direction, the crowd in her peripheral vision was a major distraction. She just couldn't *focus.* Not like this.

Ian must have realized from her frozen expression and her stiff limbs that she wasn't able to overcome the prying eyes. He turned away from her and waved his hand at their audience.

"Clear the studio," he said to the spectators. But because Ian never asked for privacy, no one moved.

"Now!" he barked loudly.

Jordan watched, relieved, as the crowd disappeared behind the divider. Violet emerged from her room with a curious look on her face.

"Take the rest of the day," Ian said when he noticed her standing at the edge of the set.

"For real?" Violet asked, surprised.

He nodded. "Do me a favor. Make sure everyone leaves. I want it quiet and private. Got it?"

"Got it." Violet slid one last suspicious, slit-eyed look at Jordan before she spun on her spiked heels and disappeared.

Ian waited until he heard Violet's echoing heels reach the door. When it shut behind her, he turned his attention back to Jordan.

"Now," he said as he walked toward her. "No more excuses."

"Thanks for that." She felt herself immediately relax. She would've thought that having others around would make her feel *less* nervous around Ian, but now that they were alone together, she felt more at ease.

"I take it you don't do that very often," she added.

"I've never done that," Ian said as he scanned through the photographs he had already taken of her. "Not for anyone."

"Then why'd you do it for me?"

He walked over to where she was standing, and she liked his natural, long-legged swagger.

"I'm going to be blunt so we can move this along, okay?"

"Sure," she said with a shrug.

"You interest me. Individually, your features are… ordinary, but together…" He paused as he studied her face. "But together, they are extraordinary. And I feel compelled to capture that in a photograph. Fair enough?"

Jordan wrinkled her brow and gave a small shake of her head. "Was there a compliment in there somewhere? 'Cause it sure didn't sound like it…"

"You seemed like someone who'd rather get it straight. Was I wrong about that?"

"No. You're right. I'd rather get it straight."

"So…is there a problem?"

Jordan put one hand on her hip and felt her proverbial hackles rise. "I don't have a problem."

"Good." Ian nodded his head. "I'm glad to hear it. Time is money and I'd like to get back to work."

"Sure." She frowned at him. "Why not? It's your time to waste. Good luck with getting a usable shot…."

"When it comes to getting the shot," he replied with the confidence of a man who didn't often fail. "I don't need luck."

Chapter Four

Now that they were alone, and Ian had removed the distractions, he was determined to get down to business. At first her nerves, natural awkwardness and heightened self-consciousness made her feel as stiff as an overly starched shirt. But bit by bit, little by little, he coaxed her out of her shell. He was totally relaxed and in charge when he had that camera in his hand. He knew exactly what he needed to say, knew exactly how he needed to say it in order to get her to perform. The calm timbre of his voice combined with the continual stream of encouraging words stripped away the last threads of nervousness from her body. Once she shook off those nerves, she was able to feel the energy that was flowing between them; when he moved, she moved. It was a dance—a sensual, flirtatious dance. And surprisingly, being the focus of Ian's camera was nearly as exhilarating as street racing her Ducati. She hadn't expected it, wouldn't have imagined it, but modeling for Ian *excited* her.

Ian stepped closer to her. "Beautiful, Jordan. Now I want you straight on to the camera. Remember to bring your personality to the shot—a gorgeous face is only half the battle. That's it. Hold that right there."

Ian snapped off several more shots before he lowered the camera. "Are you up for a couple more?"

Her body was flooded with feel-good endorphins and her defenses were completely down. Jordan felt flushed all over her body as she smiled at him. "Sure."

Ian felt encouraged by the fact that Jordan wasn't ready to stop the session. "Up till now, I've been directing you. Now I want to see you direct yourself."

Her eyebrows lifted in surprise. Hands on hips, she asked, "Seriously?"

"Seriously." Ian smiled back at her, revealing a dimple. "Show me what you've got."

Ian found that he was thoroughly enjoying photographing Jordan. She was everything he had imagined she would be—and much, much more.

"Okay," she said with a shrug. "I can do that."

Ian lifted his camera.

"You want me to start now?" she asked.

"Whenever you're ready." He made some adjustments to the camera.

Jordan took in a deep breath and held her hands out in front of her. "Okay." She shook her head. "I can't believe I'm going to do this, but I'm going to show you something *no one*—other than my roommate and maybe the Peeping Tom next door—has ever seen before."

"That sounds promising," Ian said, and then asked teasingly, "Will I see it sometime today?"

"Hey…" Jordan teased him back. "What you're about to see takes some mental preparation. Okay?"

"By all means," he said with mock seriousness. "Prepare."

Jordan drew another deep breath and brought her hands together in the prayer position in front of her chest. "I call what you are about to see Joan Jett meets Billy Idol meets Lita Ford. Can you dig it?"

"I'm ready to be impressed." Ian bantered with her as he raised his camera and prepared to capture her poses.

Ian was like a snake charmer. He had managed to make her feel so completely comfortable that she was willing to make a fool out of herself and strike every "cool" rocker chick pose she had ever come up with in front of the bathroom mirror. Ian took picture after picture, and by the time Jordan struck her last pose, which featured her best Billy Idol snarl, she couldn't stop herself from laughing. She tilted her head back, crossed her arms in front of her stomach and laughed out loud.

"That's it!" she said dramatically. "You've taken it all out of me. I've got nothing left to give."

Ian realized that he was laughing along with her. The rare sound of his own laughter seemed strange and out of place in the studio. But with Jordan, laughing seemed like the most natural thing to do.

"You brought the magic, Jordan. There's no doubt about it." He played along with her as he walked over to the computer. "Why don't you go get changed while I start to review the images. I definitely want you to take a look at these before you go—I think you're going to be surprised."

Jordan rushed to change into her own top so she could hurry back to Ian. She was nervous and excited to see the finished product. Was it possible that he'd managed to get usable shots of her? Rent and painting supplies were hanging in the balance. She checked her reflection in the mirror one last time before she returned. On the short round trip to Ian's side, a sharp sense of humiliation began to creep into her system. Without knowing why she had felt compelled to do it, she had let her guard down and showed him the silly, private side that only her close friends and family had ever seen. Not only had she shown that side to him, she had actually let him capture it with his camera! As she walked over to him, she wished she could press Rewind and take back the last fifty frames.

"What's the verdict?" she asked with feigned bravado as she joined Ian at the computer. Nonchalantly, he switched places with her so she was standing to his right before he clicked on one of his favorite shots.

"Some of the images we got at the end are ridiculously good. Just look at this one." He pointed to a shot of her giving him her Billy Idol snarl. She stared at the pictures on the screen wordlessly, and after a second or two, Ian prodded her impatiently. "Well? What do you think?"

Jordan shook her head slowly, transfixed by the photographs. The woman staring back at her didn't resemble her at all. That woman looked as if she belonged in front of a camera.

"I can't believe it," she finally said. "I actually look…"

"Beautiful? Edgy? Badass?"

"Well…I wouldn't go that far—"

"I would," Ian declared.

"But I look *good*. Really good."

"You have very complicated angles, but that's what's so exciting about your face," he explained as he clicked on another of his favorite shots. "Look at this. See how the light is reflecting from your cheekbone? You can actually see the structure of your face and appreciate the beauty.

Now here…" Ian switched photos. "Look at this one. Your face is in shadow and your beauty is lost."

"So…what you're saying is that I have a tricky face to photograph?"

"That's *exactly* what I'm saying! But with the right lighting, with the right photographer, your face photographs like a dream." Ian looked down at her with a pleased smile. "You're a natural."

Jordan couldn't believe what she was seeing. One amazing shot after another. She actually *looked* like a model, and for the first time in her life she enjoyed seeing herself in a photograph. And she felt so good about the results that she brushed aside her humiliation and allowed herself to enjoy the moment.

"I've gotta admit I'm blown away," she said to him. "I haven't seen a decent picture of myself since I was in elementary school."

Ian stared down at Jordan and couldn't remember the last time he had been so intrigued by a woman. It wasn't just her gorgeous face. It was more than that. He couldn't quite put his finger on it, but he knew instinctively that he had never met anyone like Jordan Brand before. She was a quirky combination of innocent sensuality and edgy attitude. She lacked the purely superficial obsession that most models in his acquaintance possessed. But then, she wasn't a model, was she? She was something entirely new. Something entirely different. And she was the woman he needed to create the final book that he envisioned. Now all he had to do was get her under contract.

"Let's go up front and talk about the project," Ian said.

Jordan followed him to the front of the studio; he gestured to one side of the couch. "Can I get you something to drink?"

Now that her adrenaline was starting to drop back to

normal levels, she was reminded about the excesses the night before. Her stomach was upset and her head was pounding.

"Water'd be good," Jordan said, and then as an afterthought, "Do you have an aspirin or something in the same general analgesic family?"

"Still feeling lousy from last night?"

She nodded as she perched on the edge of the couch. "Note to self. Beware of the pink-champagne fountain. Of course, I admit that I'm a bit of a lightweight. I'm usually the designated driver."

Ian returned with a highball glass filled with fizzing water. "What were you celebrating?" He held out the glass to her. "Here. Drink this."

"Bachelorette party." Jordan took the glass. She wrinkled her nose and smelled the liquid. "What is it?"

"Drink it quick. Before the fizzing stops," he instructed.

She made a face. "What is it?"

"Brioschi."

"What?"

"Brioschi. It's an antacid. My mom swore by it. If I had an upset stomach when I was a kid, that's what I got."

When Jordan still hesitated, Ian repeated, "It's an antacid, I swear. I'm not slipping you a roofie. Drink it before it stops fizzing or it won't work," he added when Jordan continued to stare at it.

"All right, bossy. Geez." She brought the glass up to her mouth.

"Drink it all down at once."

Jordan raised her eyebrows at him. "I will. Give me a minute to emotionally prepare myself."

She reached up and pinched her nose as she gulped the liquid down. After she was done, she coughed a few times. "*That* was disgusting."

"It'll cure what ails you. Guaranteed."

"Couldn't you give me something to chase it with at least?" Jordan held out the empty glass to him.

"It's not a shot, it's an antacid." He took the glass and with a smile in his voice said, "You're welcome."

"Thank you." The words were laced with her trademark sarcasm. "Were you trying to cure me or kill me?"

Ian returned from the kitchen, sat down on the couch, stretched out his long legs with one ankle over the other. He rested his head on his hand as he looked at her. "That's a new one. I've never heard of death by antacid before."

"There's a first time for everything, GQ." Jordan's lips quirked up into a smile.

"I bet you're feeling better already." He nodded his head toward her.

She thought about it before she responded. "You know what? I *do* feel a little better. That stuff's a miracle drug."

"Told you."

Jordan studied Ian for a moment. "You know…I thought you'd be a lot different."

"What did you think I'd be like?" he asked. Then he held up his hand. "No, wait. Let me try to fill in the blanks." He raised his pointer finger. "Arrogant."

Jordan nodded and shrugged one shoulder in agreement.

Ian held up another finger. "Egotistical."

She nodded again.

He held up a third finger. "Womanizer."

"That's a pretty comprehensive list. You must've heard it all before," Jordan said. In truth, he had hit all the major headings she had labeled him with. Maybe she had judged him too harshly too soon.

"I get how people view me because of the business I'm in. I don't agree with it, but I don't have the time to dwell on it. It is what it is."

"And your looks," Jordan said. "People judge you for that, too, I suppose."

"That was just the luck of the genetic lottery," Ian said with an irritated shrug. "But you're right. That's part of it. Still, people who know me, people who work with me... know that I'm always thinking about the next amazing image. I genuinely love the art form of photography. And, honestly, the rest of the stuff that comes with the job is just white noise to me."

"I can respect that." Jordan nodded, surprised that she actually had something in common with him. "You're a perfectionist. I'm a perfectionist about my artwork, too."

"Are you a tattoo artist?"

"What?" she asked, confused. Then she remembered where they had first met. "No. I'm a painter. Starving, of course—what else, right? But there's a fine-arts gallery downtown that's sponsoring me. I have my first show starting February 1, so hopefully the starving part will change."

Ian nodded as he listened to her. "So how are you making ends meet until the show?"

"I bartend at Altitude on the weekends," Jordan said. "And every once in a while I sell one of my designs as tattoo flash to Marty or Chappy. That's what I was doing the day that we met. I have kind of a small following in the underground music and art scene. One of my friends wanted me to design her tattoo and it took off from there. After a bunch of my friends went to him asking for my artwork, Marty offered me a deal. He does his own custom work, of course, but if someone wants one of my designs as a tattoo, they have to go to his shop to get it, and I get a cut. It's a pretty sweet deal for me, but the money's not nearly regular enough to keep me in canvases and paint, I can tell you that much."

Ian leaned forward and rested his forearms on his

thighs. "Then I'd say I have pretty impeccable timing. Because if you agree to model for me, you'll be able to buy supplies for this show and the next. Isn't that right?"

Jordan pushed a wayward lock of hair back off her forehead. "I can't deny that you have a point. I could really use the money right now."

"Then let's talk business, Jordan." Ian sat upright. "I really want you for this project. I can't say it any plainer than that. I like what I saw today—you're a natural in front of the camera and you've got great instincts for someone who hasn't modeled professionally." He lifted his eyebrows. "So? What do you think? Do you want the gig?"

Jordan studied him intently. She crossed her arms over her chest and hunched her shoulders a bit. Part of her wanted to jump at the chance. She needed the money and she'd had a blast modeling today. But there was something inside of her that was making her hesitate.

"What's holding you back from saying yes?" Ian asked. "Is it me? Do I make you nervous?"

"I don't know. Maybe." She shrugged noncommittally. "But it's not like you're going to go all *Silence of the Lambs* on me."

"Then what?" Ian stood up and walked over to one of the copper barrels that were being used as decorative tables. He moved the catalogs aside and sat down so he was directly across from her. "Look, Jordan. I really want us to work together. Tell me what I can do to help you get to yes."

"Well. I'm from Montana…" she said slowly.

"Okay."

"And I was raised to believe that if something *seems* too good to be true, then it *is* too good to be true. You catch my drift?"

"Sure," Ian said. "You think there's a catch."

"Exactly. A famous photographer tracks *me* down?"

Jordan pointed to her chest. "And wants to pay me twenty-five thousand dollars to model for him? I mean, come on—what're the chances, really?"

"Okay." Ian breathed in through his nose and then let out the breath. "I think I get what's holding you back."

"And what have you come up with, oh, Obi Wan?" she asked with a combination of sarcasm and skepticism.

"You think that I have an ulterior motive," he said as he watched her carefully.

Jordan was unlike any other woman he'd ever met—a rare gem in a sea of semiprecious stones. And he knew instinctively that she needed to be handled with care if he wanted to get her under contract for the book. Unfortunately, he couldn't rely on his usual bag of tricks—she wasn't impressed with his fame, his money or his connections. And unlike most women, who he typically had to pry off his couch with a crowbar, Jordan looked as if she might try to bolt at the slightest provocation. She reminded him of a beautiful, untamed mare, wild and unpredictable. He had absolutely no idea how to handle her. And that only intrigued him more. It made him want her under contract even more.

"Well?" she asked pointedly. "Do you?"

"Listen, Jordan. The only thing I can do right now is tell you how things work with me. As a general rule, I don't get involved with the women I photograph. I've learned through trial and error that professional boundaries make for a low-drama life. So when I tell you that I want you for my book, I don't have a hidden agenda. You'll have a contract, and when you're done, you'll have twenty-five thousand dollars in the bank. I'll have the images I need for my book, and you'll have plenty of spending money in your pockets to go wild at the art-supply store. We both get what we want."

The man had a way with persuasion; there was no doubt about that. Ian was sitting close enough to her that she could see every perfect feature of his face, from his golden skin and strong, determined jawline to his perfectly sculpted nose and lips. He was a walking billboard for what a healthy, handsome, all-American male should be. And, shockingly, she wasn't repelled by his rock-hard body and handsome face, as she normally would be. In Ian's case, she was atypically drawn to him, like a moth to a flame.

Before Jordan could say, "Let me think about it," Ian glanced at his watch as said, "Look, I've got to start getting ready to head out of town on Monday. Why don't we do this—I'll have my attorney send you the contract via email. You left your information with Violet, right?"

Jordan nodded. This would give her time to think about Ian's job offer with her head and not her impulses. She had a bad habit of making snap decisions, and often lived to regret them.

"Take a look at the contract—get an attorney to look it over—and if you're interested, you've got a job waiting for you with me. But the ball's in your court now, okay?" Ian offered her his hand.

"That sounds like a plan." Jordan slipped her hand into his. As his warm skin touched hers, a spark of electricity jumped between them. Surprised, she looked down at their hands and then up into his face. She could tell by his expression that he had felt the spark as well, but instead of pulling his hand away, he held on to hers and gently squeezed her fingers. Just for a moment, before he let her hand slip away.

Wordlessly, Ian opened the door that led into the reception area, and then in three long strides reached the outer door and opened it for her, as well. Jordan's arm brushed against his shoulder as she stepped into the hallway, and the faint scent of his cologne lingered in her senses as she pushed the down arrow for the elevator. After it lit up, she turned to face him.

"I hope you seriously consider my offer, Jordan. You and me—we can make beautiful art together."

"I think I'd like that, Ian," she said honestly.

Neither of them spoke as the elevator made its way upward. As she heard the sound of it approaching the third floor, she said, "I'd like to ask you something before I go."

"Shoot." Ian appeared completely relaxed and confident as he leaned back against the doorjamb.

"Tell me the truth…. Don't you think it was wrong, hunting me down the way you did?"

"No." He didn't hesitate in answering. "I don't. When I want something, I go after it. And I want you."

"Do you always get what you want, GQ?"

"Not always." A dimple appeared in his right cheek when he smiled at her. "Usually."

"Do you think you're going to get what you want with me?" Jordan heard the slightly flirtatious undertone of her question.

"I have no idea," he said as he contemplated her. "But I certainly hope so."

The doors to the elevator slid open and Jordan stepped inside. She turned to face him again, but for once decided to hold her tongue. This man seemed to be able to read her like a book, and she wanted to close the cover before he saw too much.

"Until next time, Jordan."

"See you around, GQ." She flashed him a peace sign just before the doors slid silently shut.

As the elevator descended to street level Jordan discovered she couldn't seem to keep from smiling. The truth was she enjoyed going toe-to-toe with Ian. He was a worthy opponent, which was hard to find. Most guys she met were just too bendable to be fun. She had been raised around rugged Montana ranchers and she had to admit that she was tired of mushy males who were easy to push around. If she pushed Ian, she had a feeling that he wouldn't budge. He was a solid brick wall that wouldn't give an inch. He was confident, totally male and relentless in his pursuit of what he wanted. At the moment, *she* was what Ian Sterling wanted. And she was going to make damn sure she enjoyed the ride while it lasted.

Chapter Five

Ian waited a few minutes before he stepped back into his studio. First, he printed his favorite Jordan Brand photograph and then he poured himself a Scotch neat. He took both items back to his favorite spot on the couch. While he slowly savored the biting taste of the Scotch, he stared at Jordan's face. She did have a tough face to photograph well. But he had the eye and the talent to transform her unusual angles into digital magic. In all the years he had been making a living as a photographer, he had never felt as if he had a muse before. Until now. Until Jordan. She made him feel like a teenage boy about to get laid for the first time. She made him feel *alive* in a way that was completely foreign to him. There had been something magnetic between them. He hoped that Jordan had felt it, too.

Ian put the photograph down on the couch next to him, leaned his head back and closed his eyes. Working always kept his mind occupied, but in the quiet, when he was alone, that was when the physical ramifications of his failing eyesight hit home. He placed the heels of his hands on his eyes and pressed gently. It was exhausting to concentrate on viewing the world from his stronger right eye when his blurred left eye was still trying to focus in on everything around him. Like every other challenge that Stargardt had brought into his life, the constant attempt by his left eye to focus, while his right eye did all the heavy lifting, was something he just had to learn to cope with and work around. But it wore him down. And it pissed him off.

Ian was still resting his eyes when Dylan walked through the door, dropped his keys on the counter and opened the refrigerator. "What's up, brother?"

Ian looked over at him through squinted eyes. "I found her."

Dylan pulled a bottle of water from the refrigerator and twisted off the top. "The chick on the motorcycle?"

"Jordan." Ian nodded as he held out the photograph. "I took this today."

Dylan studied Jordan's face for a few seconds before he handed the photograph back. "You're right—she's got an interesting look. Great eyes, great cheekbones. I'm not sure I would've chased her down the street, but whatever blows up your skirt."

"*Interesting?* That's how you would describe her? Maybe I'm not the only one around here going blind." Ian shook his head at his partner's lack of artistic vision. "I could name *twenty* seasoned models who can't deliver like this."

"Hey—it's your book. If she's the one you want, I'm all for it." Dylan walked around the couch and put his bottle of water on one of the hammered copper barrels. He pulled the barrel over to an art-deco chair and sat down. "God, I hate these stupid barrels. And this stupid chair.

Why did you agree to buy all of this artsy-fartsy junk in the first place?"

"Hey." Ian held up his hand. "Don't put that off on me. I was trying to be nice to your girlfriend."

Dylan put his foot up on the barrel. "*Ex*-girlfriend. And she dropped out of design school for a reason, you know."

"It's a little late to start complaining about it now."

Dylan nodded. "You're right. It is. Did you see that Chelsea put in her two weeks'?"

"Yeah. I tried to talk her out of it. I apologized. But sometimes you just can't unring a bell."

"Do you want me to start looking for a replacement right away or do you want me to wait?" Dylan's eyes zoned in on Ian's glass.

"I'd rather wait until I get back from the Elite Jewelers job," Ian said, before he polished off his Scotch.

"All right. So what're you drinking there, partner?"

"Scotch," Ian said unapologetically.

Dylan glanced at his Rolex. "Getting a bit of an early start?"

Ian put his glass down on the end table. "How am I supposed to know what time it is when I have to keep the blinds shut all the time?" He nodded to the closed plantation shutters. "I mean, I can either wear sunglasses indoors to cut down on my exposure to bright light. Or option B, I keep the blinds shut so I have the fun of going blind more *slowly*." There was an unmistakable bitterness in his voice as he continued. "And what's completely ironic about this is that I actually *bought* this place for the windows! Not that it does me a bit of good now. Photographers spend their careers chasing the light, right?" Ian shook his head in disgust. "Let me ask you this—what good's a photographer who has to hide from it?"

Dylan didn't know exactly how to respond. It was difficult to know what to say to Ian these days. They had been best friends since high school and he had never seen his friend in this kind of shape. Ever since his diagnosis, Ian had changed. He was angry. Easily frustrated. Closed off. The Ian Dylan used to know didn't wallow in self-pity and was annoyed when others around him did. But this new Ian had turned self-pity into an art form. The problem was that Ian couldn't see it; he thought he was handling it just fine.

"Well, it seems like you've come up with a really great solution," Dylan said in a frustrated tone. "Drink yourself into oblivion."

Ian stood up and marched over to the bar. He poured himself another drink and belted it down, then waved his empty glass at him. "What do you know about it, Dylan? What do you think you know about *any* of this? There's only one of us going blind in this room—isn't that right?"

Dylan didn't respond immediately. After a moment he said, "You're my partner and my friend. This impacts me, too. You've just been too self-absorbed to notice."

"Self-*absorbed?*" Ian asked incredulously. "Of course I'm self-absorbed! I'm fighting for my life here!"

"I don't see you fighting, Ian. From where I'm sitting, it looks like you're giving in and giving up. I love you like a brother and I've gotta tell you—I'm worried about you."

"Well, don't be." Ian leaned over the bar with his hands flat against the marble countertop. "I've got it all under control."

"Is that right?"

"That's right."

"You're flat-out lying to yourself if you think that's true, Ian. You've completely closed yourself off from everyone in your life, including me. You've broken things off with Shelby."

Ian shook his head slightly. "She broke it off with me."

"Of course she did!" Dylan gave a sharp laugh. "I don't doubt that you backed her into a corner so tight that she had *no choice* but to dump you."

Ian crossed his arms over his chest. "She wants kids and I'm not going to give her any. I did her a favor...now she's free to go find someone who will."

Dylan took his feet off the table and leaned forward. "Okay—so forget Shelby. I always thought she was your rebound relationship anyway. But that doesn't change the fact that you're screwing up, and I'm the only one around here whose gonna be honest with you about it. You're not taking care of yourself and I'm telling you, man, shoving your head in a bottle of Scotch isn't the answer."

"How do you know?" Ian held his glass in place as he carefully poured himself another drink.

Dylan rubbed his hands over his face with a sigh. "What did that shrink of yours say about all this?"

"Just a bunch of psychological mumbo jumbo." He waved his hand in the air. "I'm not going back."

"But what did she say?"

"That I'm grieving my old life, duh, and *apparently* I'm stuck in three—count them, *three*—of the five stages of grief. But great news," Ian added sarcastically. "Once I get to the fifth stage everything'll be copacetic and I'll feel just fine about the whole going-blind thing. Something to look forward to...."

"Which stages?"

"Anger, denial, depression...."

"Sounds about right." Dylan nodded.

"Well, thank you for your input, Dr. Freud."

After a short silence between them, Dylan took a breath and let it out before he spoke again. "You know what, Ian? I've been watching you run this thing off into a ditch for a while now, and I've tried to back off and give you your space, because let's face it—you got the short end of the stick here. But we need to move forward and figure out how to keep our business on track."

Ian put his now empty glass on the bar. "I already told you what I want to do about the business."

Dylan displayed a rare show of temper. "*What?* To just let the business *fail?* What kind of lame-ass idea is *that,* Ian? We've got too much time and money invested in this company just to piss it all away."

"Do you think I want that? Do you?" He raised his voice as he pointed to his eyes. "I'm losing my eyesight! Didn't you get the memo?"

Dylan took in another deep breath, exhaled and forced himself to lower his tone. The truth was, he had been avoiding this fight for too long. He had been tiptoeing around Ian and it was time to sort some things out between them. But he also knew his friend well enough to back off before he completely shut down.

"From what I understand…" Dylan said calmly. "From what I've read, you aren't going to lose your peripheral vision. We can *work* with that."

Ian sank back down into the couch. "Dylan. Let's get real about this thing. Do you have any idea how many of our clients are going to bail once word gets out about this? I'm telling you, there isn't a client out there who's going to beat down the door to put millions of dollars of campaign money into a half-*blind* photographer's hands." Almost as an afterthought, he added, "Tell me I'm wrong."

"No." Dylan dragged his fingers through his sun-bleached, light brown hair. "I don't think you're wrong."

"Then what exactly do you have in mind?"

"We evolve."

"Into what?"

"A consulting firm. A full-blown modeling agency."

Dylan paused before he added, "We could even eventually hire some photographers and train them *your* way. Photographers would line up around the block to learn the Ian Sterling method. I mean, *come on,* man. *Anything's* better than just giving up and throwing in the towel."

Ian rubbed his palm over the back of his neck as he considered Dylan's words. From the minute he'd heard the diagnosis he had been determined to close shop when his eyes got too bad for him to work as a photographer. But maybe he was wrong about that. Maybe there was a way to keep the company alive.

"I don't know," he finally said. "Maybe you have a point. Maybe I need to consider our options. But I'm telling you that I just don't want to be bothered with this right now. I still have enough vision to get by and all I want is to get this next job out of the way so I can focus full-time on the book. Once I've shot it, we'll sit down and figure out what our next step should be. Fair enough?"

Dylan studied him for several seconds. "And until then you'll start taking better care of yourself. Follow doctor's orders—lay off the booze."

"Yes. *Jesus.* You know what? Who needs a wife when I already have a nag like you?" Ian said with a frustrated sigh. He picked up the picture of Jordan that he had set on the table and ran his hand lightly over her face.

Dylan nodded toward the picture. "And you're sure she's the one for the book? Does she even have any modeling experience?"

"Who needs experience with a face like this?" Ian asked rhetorically. "And, yeah—I'm sure. Just look at her. She eats the lens with her eyes. She's a natural." He added more quietly, "She…inspires me. I know she can deliver."

It was the way he was talking about Jordan that caught Dylan off guard. He hadn't seen Ian excited about a model in a long time. He watched his friend closely as Ian continued to speak.

"You know, the only time I feel normal anymore is when I'm behind the camera. Everything in my life has changed—every day of my life is a constant trial in how I'm going to work around this…idiotic disease. I feel like Stargardt is slowly robbing me of my life—bit by bit, day by day—until eventually it'll take everything away from me. My work, my independence, my future… There are a lot of days when I dread waking up, and I have to force myself to get out of bed and face another day living like this. But…" He stared down at Jordan's face. "When I discover someone like her—when I *photograph* someone like her—for that short period of time, I'm not Ian with the screwed-up eyes anymore. I'm just Ian Sterling, photographer."

It took a minute for Dylan to realize the magnitude of what his friend had just said. It had been a really long time since Ian had opened up to him about anything, much less something so personal. And it made him wonder if the change he saw in him could be directly linked to Jordan.

"I haven't heard you talk about anyone like this since…" Dylan stopped himself before he said Ian's ex-fiancée's name.

Ian laid Jordan's picture on his thigh. "Lexi."

"Sorry, man—I didn't mean to bring her up."

Ian felt his gut clench as it always did when he thought of Alexia. He had fallen hard for her when they'd met on a photo shoot. She was a gorgeous up-and-coming stylist with a larger-than-life personality. After an intense, passionate, bicoastal courtship, he had asked her to marry him. He'd always wanted the wife, the kids, the white picket fence, and he had believed that Lexi was the one woman he could spend the rest of his life loving. But the diagnosis shortly followed the engagement, and Lexi's wedding planning began to taper off. It didn't take her long to figure out that she didn't want to be married to a once-famous blind photographer. She called off the wedding, and the only time he had seen her in the past four years was when they worked on the same campaign. The truth was, being unceremoniously dumped by Lexi after his diagnosis still stung.

"Hey—I forgot to tell you." Dylan tried to steer the conversation away from her. "I heard back from the folks at the Midway museum and we've got our pick of several dates for the shoot."

"You know…" Ian continued on the subject of Lexi. "I can't really blame her for bailing on me. Who would want to chain herself to a washed-up photographer without a driver's license?"

"You have a chauffeur—you don't need to drive." Dylan tried to make a joke of the fact that Ian would eventually have to give up his license. "And as far as Lexi goes, she turned out to be a social-climbing gold digger who latched on to you because of what she thought you could do for her career. I know that's harsh, but that's the truth, brother. And if you ask me, you're lucky you found out when you did. The last thing you needed was a nasty divorce—and with Lexi, you'd better know it would've been nothing *but* nasty. The only good thing I can say about Lexi is that she hasn't *blogged* about what's going on with you. I give her credit for that, but that's the only thing I can give her credit for…."

When Ian didn't respond, Dylan added, "And you know what? I'm really glad to hear you get excited about this new model. You need to forget about the past and focus on what's ahead of you." He hesitated before saying, "Because let's face it. Between this thing with your eyes and all the B.S. Lexi put you through, you've been in a rut. I'd really like you to consider rejoining the living."

"I *have* been living," Ian said defensively. "I've been working."

"There's more to life than work. Why don't you come over tomorrow for a change? We're gonna be grilling out. Jenna has some smokin' hot girlfriends who live in bikinis...."

"I don't know," Ian said. It was hard for him to be surrounded by people he didn't know. It was too hard to keep up with new faces; too hard to keep everyone on his right side without being obvious about it. Before Stargardt, he would've been the first one at the party. Now he couldn't remember the last time he'd gotten together with friends. "I'll think about it."

"Sure you will." Dylan shook his head.

"I'm serious. I'll think about it. Okay?"

"Okay. But I'd really like you to come over. We haven't hung out in a really long time." Dylan crushed the empty water bottle in his hand. "Hey, why don't you invite this new girl? She looks like she knows how to have a good time...."

"No. You know I like to try to keep it strictly business with the models. Besides, Jordan hasn't signed the contract yet. The last thing I want to do is give her a reason to say no."

"Yeah, I suppose you have a point." Dylan stood up and walked over to Ian. He reached out and clasped his hand. "But sometimes you've gotta take a risk, change the rules. You know what I mean?"

"We'll see," Ian said. But the truth was he couldn't imagine any woman—especially a young, vibrant woman like Jordan—taking on his load of baggage. He just couldn't see it happening.

"All right, brother—I'm out." Dylan paused at the door. "I'll see you tomorrow, right?"

"Sure," Ian said. "You bet."

Jordan was excited when Ian contacted her late Sunday night to set up a meeting for the next morning. The man really didn't waste any time. He was determined, focused and aggressive. She liked that about him. In fact, she *admired* that about him. As it turned out, Ian Sterling was more than just a handsome face that used to hang on her bedroom wall. He was a force to be reckoned with.

She had received a draft of her contract via email mid-Sunday morning, which she had promptly forwarded to her twin, Josephine, who was attending her first year of law school. Once Jo gave her the green light, Jordan emailed Ian and agreed to sign. By Monday morning, she was heading back to his studio.

Jordan was surprised when the door was opened by a petite, slender blonde in a tailored, pin-striped suit. The woman's shiny hair was pulled back into a severe chignon that emphasized her strong cheekbones and heavily lashed, moss-green eyes. She didn't smile at Jordan, but extended her hand.

"Good morning, Miss Brand. My name is Shelby Payton. I'm Mr. Sterling's attorney. Please come in."

Shelby had a distinctively honey-dipped Southern drawl that wasn't often heard in California.

"You sound like you're from Georgia," Jordan said as she followed her into the loft.

Shelby looked over her shoulder, but kept walking. "Savannah. Born and bred."

"What brought you to California?" Jordan felt conspicuous next to the little Georgia peach. She stood head and shoulders above her and felt like a gangly giraffe lumbering behind a graceful gazelle.

"Ian, actually." The bite in Shelby's tone when she said his name was a hairline crack in her otherwise flawless exterior.

Ignoring the bait the attorney had thrown her way, Jordan changed the subject and said, "My twin just started law school."

Shelby stopped at the bottom of the metal stairs leading to the second floor of the loft and sent her a forced, plastic smile. "How nice for her."

Nobody could really fault her tone, smile or words, but Jordan had no trouble figuring out that Shelby had her claws out.

"Mr. Sterling. Miss Brand has arrived."

"And on time, too…." Ian appeared at the top of the stairs. "Did I hear you say something about a twin?"

"Yes. I have a twin sister. Josephine. She's studying law at Berkeley."

Now Ian was standing next to her. He was fresh out of the shower and she couldn't stop herself from breathing in the clean, soapy scent that clung to his skin.

"Fraternal or identical?" he asked, and she could tell by the look on his face that he was pleased she had showed.

Jordan laughed up at him. She had no idea why she was so happy to see him. "Mirror, actually. Which is why she's always been the photogenic one. But don't get any ideas. Trust me…. She'd go all Van Gogh on you and lop off an ear before she'd agree to be a model. The only thing she wanted for her tenth birthday was a signed photograph of Gloria Steinem, and she nearly set the barn on fire burning her training bra when she was eleven. Not model material, if you get my drift."

"It's not a subtle message." Ian smiled down at her.

"Shall we get started?" Shelby was curt. "I have another early appointment."

Once they got down to business, the attorney was efficient and professional as she reviewed the body of the contract. When they reached the last page, and Jordan had signed and dated for the last time, Shelby opened her briefcase, slipped the signed contract inside, withdrew an envelope and then snapped the briefcase shut. She handed Jordan the envelope as she stood up.

"I'll have my secretary send you a PDF copy of the signed contract via email today. Now, if you'll excuse me, I do have another meeting." She spun away on her Manolo Blahnik shoes, but paused in the doorway. "And, Jordan?"

Jordan pulled her eyes away from the check inside the envelope. "Yes?"

"Good luck with Ian. You're gonna need it."

Caught off guard, Jordan found her brain seizing up and she couldn't think of a snappy retort. Ian caught her eye briefly, his lips thinned with displeasure, before he followed Shelby into the waiting area.

"Hey," he said in a lowered voice. "What was that little tantrum all about, Shelby? It was your idea to stay on as my attorney after we ended things. But I can see now that this isn't going to work. Someone else at the firm needs to handle my business from now on."

"Fine with me." She swung open the door. "I'll have my secretary transfer your files to another attorney in the firm and send you a final bill."

Jordan heard the outer door to the studio slam shut as Ian reappeared.

"Listen, Jordan…about what Shelby just said."

Jordan shook her head quickly. "Hey, don't worry about it. Whatever *that* was, it's none of my business."

"Breaking up is a royal pain in the neck," Ian muttered under his breath.

Instead of responding to his statement, Jordan pointed to his cell phone on the table. "You missed a call."

He strode over to it, slipped on his reading glasses and then picked up his phone. Jordan began to stand up, not wanting to intrude, but he waved her down. Without a word, he dialed the missed number and then brought the phone up to his ear.

"You did *what?* Jesus, Mandy—we're scheduled to start shooting tomorrow! What were you thinking?"

Ian paused to listen to the person at the other end of the line. "It's great you made bail, but what good does that do me? You can't leave the state now, much less the country. I just don't understand how you can be this *irresponsible.* You knew I was counting on you for this shoot. The client requested you!" There was another pause and then Ian said angrily, "No. Stop apologizing, Mandy. You're out of a job. This conversation's over."

He ended the call, tossed his phone on the table and paced around the room with his arms crossed over his chest. Suddenly, he stopped and looked at Jordan contemplatively. After a second or two he asked, "Do you have a passport?"

"Sure." She nodded slowly. "Why?"

"I need a model," Ian said firmly. "Go home, pack your bags. I'll pick you up at your place in one hour. You're coming to Curaçao."

Chapter Six

For some inexplicable reason, Jordan had allowed Ian to turn her world upside down. Yes, she had always been spontaneous, but packing her bags and flying to a Dutch Caribbean island with a man she had just met was a little impulsive even for her. It had all happened so quickly. One minute she was signing a contract and picking up a check, and then the next minute she found herself in Ian's Bentley heading toward the executive airport. She'd sent Josephine and Amaya a heads-up text and arranged for one of the alternate bartenders to cover her shifts at Altitude. She hadn't had a chance to call the folks, but figured there'd be time for that later. She had packed in such a rush that she was certain she was missing imperative toiletries and clothing. And now that she was sitting next to Ian in his Bentley, the reality of her split-second decision was starting to sink in. She was actually leaving the country with Ian Sterling. It felt Salvador Dali surreal, no question about it. Jordan glanced over at Ian, who was talking on the phone, and all she could think was that she had completely lost her marbles.

She was still considering her sanity when they pulled into Montgomery Airfield. The chauffeur shut off the engine, jumped out and quickly opened the door for her, and when Jordan stepped out of the Bentley, she seriously considered getting right back in. But when Ian came around the back of the car, dapper in his pin-striped suit, and gave her a reassuring smile, her resistance melted away. The man just had a way of making her feel comfortable and in control, as if every decision she made with him was spot-on.

And she liked it. She liked being with him. In fact, she felt proud to be with him. He commanded attention as he walked through the small airport with his long, determined strides. From behind his amber-tinted sunglasses with the wraparound lenses, he didn't seem to notice the attention he was receiving from females of all ages as Jordan and he navigated their way through the facility. He always watched out for her, occasionally putting his hand lightly on the small of her back to guide her in front of him so she could avoid another passenger. Little by little, action by action, Ian Sterling was smashing all her preconceived notions about him.

They cleared customs in no time at all and then headed for Ian's private hangar. Inside, a small jet emblazoned with the Sterling & Axel logo awaited their arrival.

"Uh…*wow!* You have your own jet?" Jordan asked, surprised, as she rolled her bag behind her.

"I travel so much for work, it was just easier this way." Ian nodded a greeting to the pilot. "Captain Stern." The two men shook hands. "Good to see you."

"Likewise, Mr. Sterling."

"Did you get my message about the additional passenger?"

"Yes, sir. I did."

"Good." Ian nodded as he turned toward her. "Captain Stern, this is Ms. Brand."

"A pleasure, Ms. Brand." The pilot tipped his hat.

"Jordan." She shook his hand.

"Are we all set?" Ian asked as the pilot began to load their bags into the cargo space of the jet.

"Yes, sir." He closed the hatch and straightened. "Once you're settled, we'll prepare to leave. Looks like we'll have good weather all the way to Curaçao, and we should be able to get you there on time."

"That's what I like to hear," Ian said as he gestured for Jordan to board the jet.

The aircraft was professionally decorated with masculine grays and blacks combined with shiny sterling-silver accents and mahogany inlays. There were two oversize reclining chairs that faced each other on the right side of the passenger cabin, with a small table in between. A long plush couch lined the left side, with a direct view of the flat screen TV. There was soft, ambient lighting, with pull-down coverings on the windows blocking out the glare of sunlight.

"Should I sit here?" Jordan nodded to one of the chairs.

"Take the one on your right, if you don't mind," Ian said. He wanted to sit in the chair facing the pilot so his view of the couch and the cockpit wasn't blocked out by his left eye. If Jordan moved to the couch, he wanted to be able to see her.

"I don't mind." She sat down and immediately buckled her seat belt.

Ian took off his jacket and hung it up in the small closet behind his chair, then took the seat across from her. "I didn't know you were going to be joining me or I would've had the jet stocked with your favorite foods," he said. "We do have some snacks and drinks stocked. Water. Coke."

"Actually…" Jordan nervously ran her hand along the chair's armrest. Once inside, she found the jet a little too narrow, a little too claustrophobic for her liking. "Do you have anything stronger?"

"Is Scotch strong enough?"

"That'll do. On the rocks, please." Jordan wiped her damp palms off on her jeans.

"I think I'll join you," he said as he pulled a bottle and two crystal highball glasses from the small cabinets above the refrigerator. He put ice in hers and then poured his neat.

"Here you go." Ian held out the glass for her.

After he sat down again, he reached forward and touched his glass to hers. *"Salute!"*

"Do you only toast in Italian or do you speak it, as well?" Jordan asked of the toast he had made.

"I've picked up a little here and there." Ian smiled at her before he took a drink.

"Let me guess…a model you dated?" she asked with a raised eyebrow.

"Nice try. No. Not a model. A reporter." He winked at her over the rim of his glass. "She had some of the best equipment in the business."

Jordan laughed at his comment—that was the first even remotely suggestive one Ian had made to her, and she could tell by the deepening of the laugh lines around his eyes that he was starting to feel comfortable enough around her to joke. And that made her relax a little bit.

"Oh, I just bet she did." Jordan smiled back at him before she brought the amber liquid up to her lips and took a small sip. She closed her eyes as the spicy-sweet drink created a burning sensation that started in her throat and ended in her stomach. Jordan let out a long sigh before she opened her eyes. Ian was staring curiously at her.

"Everything okay?"

"Everything's fine. I can be kind of an anxious flier sometimes, that's all. And it just feels a little…cozy in here, you know?"

"Are you trying to intimate that I have a dinky jet?"

Jordan laughed. "No. Of course not. Your jet is *very* substantial."

"Thank you," Ian said with a small smile. "But all kidding aside, are you going to be okay?"

"Oh. Yeah. No worries." Jordan took another sip of her drink. "But you know what? Before I was hypnotized, I wouldn't have been able to get on a plane like this one— no way, no how."

"Really?"

"Seriously. Just the thought of getting on something this small—I mean substantial—sorry…"

"Forgiven." Ian smiled at her.

"…would've totally freaked me out."

"And hypnosis really helped you get over your fear of flying? I've always thought of hypnotists as snake-oil salesmen."

"Me, too!" Jordan agreed. "I was shocked when it actually worked. See—my roommate went to a hypnotherapist because she was addicted to vanilla crème doughnuts and was completely outgrowing all her clothes. So this therapist claimed that she could treat you for just about anything. If you could name it, she'd hypnotize you for it—weight loss, smoking, gambling…."

"Fear of flying."

"Exactly," Jordan said. "So the very same day my roommate was hypnotized, and I'm being totally serious about this, she was cured. One minute she's making midnight runs for doughnuts and then the next minute she's free of vanilla crème. So I figured, hey, why not give it a try. Four hundred dollars and four sessions later, I was better. Not totally fixed…." Jordan held up her glass. "Hence the liquid courage. But better."

"That's pretty impressive."

"It is." She nodded. "Who knew?"

Ian held up his glass in turn. "Well, I'm glad it worked and I'm glad you're here."

"Thank you kindly, sir," Jordan said as she finished the rest of the Scotch.

"Would you like another before we take off?"

"No." She shook her head. "Do you mind if I pull up my shade, though? That might help."

"Be my guest." Ian took both their empty glasses while Jordan slid up her window shade and looked outside.

Ian retrieved his sunglasses from his jacket and slipped them on before he sat down.

Jordan glanced over at him and noticed the glasses. "You were really serious about that whole light sensitivity thing, weren't you? Is that why all the windows are covered? Do you want me to put mine down again?"

Ian's dimple appeared as he smiled at her. "Yes, I *was* being serious when I said that I have light sensitivity. Yes, that's why the shades are closed. And no, I don't want you to close yours. I want you to be comfortable."

"Okay," Jordan said. "But if you want me to close it I will."

Before Ian could reassure her a second time, Captain Stern's voice came over the intercom and announced that they would be taxing out to the runway.

"Are you ready?" Ian asked.

"Yes." Jordan's heart began to race with a mixture of excitement and apprehension. "I'm really excited about going to Curaçao. I've been to Grand Turk, but none of the Dutch-owned islands."

"I think you'll be impressed. And, hey—don't worry about the flight there. Everything'll be fine." Ian tried to reassure her as the jet slowly taxied to the runway. "We're in good hands with Captain Stern. We've logged a lot of miles together."

Jordan closed her eyes and held on tight to the arms of her chair as the jet sped down the tarmac. Once it was safely in the air and had achieved altitude, she opened her eyes and found Ian watching her intently. No doubt he was making sure that she wasn't going to freak out on him.

She gave him a smile and a thumbs-up. "See? No worries."

Takeoffs and landings had always been the worst for her, but once they were up in the air, she felt her anxiety begin to subside. Soon the jet reached its cruising altitude and Captain Stern signaled that it was safe to move about the cabin. Jordan unbuckled her seat belt and moved over to the couch. She ran her hand over the supple leather.

"You know, my sister would be having a total fit right now, subjecting you to a lecture on carbon footprints left by private jets. And don't get me wrong—I'm concerned about the environment, too! But I've gotta admit this is pretty cool."

Ian had his chin resting in his palm as he watched her. "I'm glad you approve."

"You know what it's like?"

He shook his head, a bemused expression on his face.

"It's like being on a rerun of the *Lifestyles of the Rich and Famous* with Robin Leach."

Ian had opened his laptop, but it was more fun to watch Jordan's unabashed enjoyment of the jet than dig through hundreds of unread emails.

She pulled her phone out of her pocket and handed it to him. "Here. Do me a favor. Take my picture so I can post it on Facebook."

She slid the cover of her window shut and then sat back down on the couch. "I'd rather be able to see your eyes than have the curtain open."

"Thank you," Ian said as he pulled off his sunglasses. He closed his eyes for a moment while they adjusted to the different light. After a minute, he opened them to find Jordan watching him intently.

"That must be a real pain," she said. "Light sensitivity. Have you seen a doctor about it?"

"Many times." He held up her phone so he could take her picture. "Are you ready for your close-up?"

Jordan kicked off her shoes and sat cross-legged on the couch. "How do I look?"

"Beautiful."

He snapped the photo and then handed the phone back to her.

"Even with a crappy camera phone you still managed to make me look good," Jordan said as she looked at the picture.

"That's my job—I make beautiful women look even more beautiful."

"I'm going to put this on Facebook right now so Mom has plenty of 'freak out' time and has a chance to calm down before I call her."

Ian closed the lid of his laptop—no sense pretending that he was going to get any work done when he'd rather spend his time hanging out with Jordan. "Why would she freak out?"

"Oh—well," Jordan said as she posted the pic to her Facebook page. "I've got a really large family—I'm the youngest of five kids—and we're all kind of loud and opinionated and in each other's business all the time. I'm twenty-five but I may as well be twelve as far as my brothers are concerned. And my mom is really protective and just can't help herself from meddling in my life—it's her nature. The only ones that are pretty chill are my dad and my brother Tyler."

"You're lucky. I always wanted a big family. I was an only child," Ian said.

"Sometimes I think it would be fun to be an only child."

He shook his head. "No. It's better your way. Trust me. Now that Mom and Dad are both gone, it's just me and a sad little Cornish hen on Thanksgiving."

"You lost *both* of your parents? I'm so sorry. How long ago?"

"Dad had a heart attack when I was in high school—he went in for open-heart surgery, but he never recovered. He chain-smoked unfiltered cigarettes for years and it just wrecked his arteries. I lost my mom to breast cancer a little over a year ago."

Ian hadn't spoken to anyone about his mother since she died—not even his shrink. But speaking to Jordan about her felt right. He pulled out his wallet and showed Jordan a picture of his parents on their wedding day.

"Wow, your mom was a knockout. Your dad was really handsome, too—you look just like him."

"That's what my mom always said." Ian nodded as he put his wallet away.

"How'd they meet?"

"My mom was Danish, but she was living in Paris because she had landed a gig with Chanel—which was a coup for a model even back then. My father was stationed in France—he was a master sergeant in the army. I'm not exactly sure how he managed to wind up at the Chanel show—I think he was dating an assistant in one of the fashion houses—but either way, it was love at first sight when my father saw Mom walking down the runway. He ditched his date and waited outside the venue for nearly two hours until she came out. And the rest, as they say, is history. Of course," Ian said with a reminiscent smile, "Mom always claimed that it took her many more 'sightings' for her to fall for my dad."

"You have a great story to share with your kids one day," Jordan said. "I am really sorry that you lost both of them, though. I lost my brother Daniel about two years ago. He was a U.S. Army Ranger, and died in Iraq. I really miss him. We all really miss him. But I think my mom misses him the most."

"Maybe that's why she's so protective of you," Ian said thoughtfully.

"Could be. Makes sense." Jordan flipped through her phone and found a picture of her entire family. "Here's my twin sister, Josephine. That's my eldest brother, Luke— he's a captain in the U.S. Marines. That's Daniel before he died. And there's Mom, Dad and my middle brother, Tyler."

After Ian looked at the picture, Jordan locked her phone, slipped it into her pocket and then yawned loudly. She stretched her arms above her head. The excitement of the day had taken its toll and she suddenly felt exhausted.

"I'm really beat." She slunk down farther on the couch.

"Why don't lie down and get some rest?" Ian asked.

"You wouldn't mind?"

"No. I wouldn't mind." He stood and opened the cabinet above the couch, pulling out a pillow and blanket.

"Thank you." Jordan fluffed her pillow and covered herself with the blanket.

"You're welcome." Ian opened his laptop again and slipped on his reading glasses. "Get some rest. We have a busy couple days ahead of us."

She pulled the blanket up under her chin, but didn't immediately close her eyes. She stared at him while he started to sort through his emails.

"Ian?"

"Hmm?"

"I actually think you're a pretty good egg."

"Thank you, Jordan." He looked up from his laptop and glanced over at her. "I like you, too."

"Welcome back to the Avila Hotel, Mr. Sterling." The gentleman at the front desk seemed genuinely pleased to see Ian again.

"Thank you, Pedro. It's good to be back. Anyone else from the crew arrive early?"

"No, sir. Not yet. But a block of rooms have been set aside in the octagon wing, and of course, the Bolivar suite has been prepared for your pleasure, sir."

Ian checked them in and then rode up in the elevator with Jordan. When they reached her floor, he straddled the elevator threshold so the door wouldn't close.

"I have some things I have to do to get ready for the shoot tomorrow. You'll be okay?"

"Sure," she said. "I'm gonna get cleaned up, get settled in and order room service." She put her hand on her stomach. "I'm starved."

Ian seemed hesitant to leave her, but he eventually stepped back into the elevator as Jordan headed down the hall toward her room. Once inside, she left her bag near the door and immediately went on a hunt for the room service menu. She scanned the menu quickly before she picked up the phone and dialed.

"Yes. I'd like an order of lobster bisque, the grilled black tiger shrimp and a salad. Do you have oil and vinegar?" Jordan asked. "Great. Water's fine, with lemon, please. Thank you."

After she hung up the phone, she lifted her suitcase onto the bed nearest the balcony. During the limo ride to the hotel, Ian had told her that her roommate would arrive the next day. So for tonight, she had every intention of sprawling out and enjoying the room. And the next item on her agenda was to take a long, hot bath. She ran the bathwater, and after the tub was filled halfway, tested the temperature.

"Perfect," she said, stripping off her clothes and stepping into the tub. She immersed herself in the steamy water, closed her eyes and sighed with pleasure as the heat soothed her tired muscles. She wasn't certain how long she stayed in the tub, but by the time she heard a knock at the door, the water was tepid and her fingers were wrinkled like the skin of a raisin.

"Oh, crap!" Jordan sat up quickly, sending the water sloshing onto the floor. "Hold on!" she yelled as she slipped on the plush hotel robe. "I'm coming!"

Still damp beneath the terry robe, she quickly devoured her dinner and gulped down the water. After she popped the last bite in her mouth, Jordan grimaced as she put down her fork. Way too full, she flopped backward onto the bed and spread out her arms. Now she was completely stuffed *and* completely bored.

"Your first night in Curaçao and you're staring at a ceiling. *Alone.* Very sad."

She turned her head and looked at the hotel phone. The only person she knew in Curaçao was Ian.

Should I call the penthouse suite and see what he's doing?

"No," Jordan answered aloud. "Don't be desperate."

The calypso music drifting up from downstairs caught

her attention. She walked over to the sliding doors, pulled them open and stepped out onto the small balcony. It overlooked a beachside bar area and one of the adjacent private hotel beaches. The air was warm, but the breeze blowing in from the ocean cooled the skin of her face as she closed her eyes and let her ears tune in to the sound of the waves, barely audible over the rhythmic music.

After a moment, Jordan opened her eyes and leaned over the railing so she could get a better look at the schooner bar. The scene looked like one of those vacation commercials where people were laughing and dancing and drinking and having the best time of their lives. Jordan wanted to be *in* that commercial.

Back inside the room now, she quickly shrugged out of the robe and into a minidress with spaghetti straps and a skirt that swirled around her bare legs as she walked. She slicked her hair straight back off her face, added a touch of makeup and then used the entire bottle of gardenia lotion on her arms and freshly shaved legs. As a final touch, she slipped into a pair of strappy sandals before she inspected her reflection in a full-length mirror. She twisted to the left and then to the right.

"Not bad for jet lag, Jordy." She smiled at her reflection.

Jordan tucked her room key and ID into a small side pocket of her dress before she headed down to the bar. She smiled faintly at people as she drifted through the crowd and found her way to a stool near the crowded dance floor so she could have a good view of the band. She ordered a virgin piña colada, and when it arrived, she spun around so her back was to the bar.

Heaven.

Jordan closed her eyes and enjoyed the sexy beat of the drums and the balmy night air as it skated over her body. One hour in Curaçao and she already felt the tension slipping out of her neck and shoulders. She was having a blast in paradise, and the only thing that would make it better would be having someone to share it with.

"I'm not sure which is more beautiful…Curaçao or you."

She cringed inwardly as a male voice interrupted her blissful moment. Jordan cautiously opened her eyes and looked in the direction of the speaker. The man standing next to her was good-looking enough, with spiky brown hair and a smile that had been bleached a bright white. His cologne was too sweet, his breath too laced with liquor and his attempt to flatter her had only served to irritate her. Jordan refused his offer to buy her a drink and was grateful that he wasn't too drunk to take a hint and move on to greener pastures. Alone again, she tried to return to the wonderful Zen zone she had created before she was rudely interrupted, and silently prayed that he wasn't going to be the first in a long line of guys trolling for a one-night stand.

Just as Jordan slipped back into her Zen sweet spot, she heard another male voice beside her. But this time, her ears instantly tuned in to that silky deep baritone that could belong only to her Ian Sterling.

Chapter Seven

"It's hard to enjoy the view with your eyes closed," he said with a smile in his voice.

Jordan immediately opened her eyes and found Ian, still dressed in his suit and tie, leaning against the bar next to her. That oh-so-familiar shot of adrenaline raced through her system when she looked up into that handsome face of his.

"Hi!" She greeted him warmly with a wide smile. "You're still in your suit. You *do* realize that we're in a tropical paradise, right?"

When the bartender approached, Ian ordered water for himself and then asked her, "Do you need a refill?"

Jordan looked down at her nearly empty glass. She had polished off that drink without even thinking about it. "Virgin piña colada. Frozen, please."

After he placed the order, Ian turned back to her. "To

answer your question, yes, I'm aware that we're in paradise. But I still have work to do."

Jordan scrunched up her face. "Don't remind me. I'm freaking out about the photo shoot tomorrow."

"Don't psych yourself out. I already know that you're going to be great. Trust me, I've been in this business long enough to be able to spot raw talent."

"I'll try to relax about it," she promised. "Of course, this place makes it a whole lot easier. It's really beautiful here."

"This is one of my favorite places in the Caribbean," Ian agreed as he surveyed the moonlit waves.

"So," Jordan said. "Are you done for the night?"

He brought his eyes back to her. "Yes. I just finished meeting with hotel management. I wanted to make sure we would have full access to the grounds."

"I suppose that's a valid reason to still be walking around looking like a tax attorney."

Ian glanced down at his suit. "I think I look pretty slick in this suit."

"But of course you do."

"And I happen to think that you look beautiful in that dress." He smiled appreciatively at her.

"Thank you." Jordan grinned up at him, glad she had chosen the dress over jeans. "And it's good that you're done, because I could use the company. It's my first night in Curaçao and it would be a total bummer to spend it alone."

The bartender brought their drinks. Ian held out his glass to her for a toast. "Here's to a successful shoot."

While Jordan watched the dancers as she enjoyed her drink, Ian watched her. After his meeting with hotel management, he had decided to re-familiarize himself with the grounds and scope out some possible locations for the photo shoots. When he ventured down to the bar, he'd had no intention of staying. But then he had spotted Jordan. He had seen her and had stopped in his tracks. Part of him wanted to pretend that he hadn't noticed her and just go back to his room. But the other part of him wanted to make a beeline to her side, and that was the part that won. After watching Jordan reject one of the bar flies buzzing around her, Ian had taken his opportunity to fill the void at her side.

Jordan felt Ian's eyes on her so she looked over at him. "What?"

He didn't hesitate to respond. "I really do like you, Jordan."

"I like you too, Ian." Her reply was quick and sincere.

There was something about this moment, something about the way Ian was looking at her, that made her feel like taking a chance—taking a risk.

"Ian?"

"Hmm?"

"If I tell you something, will you promise that you won't laugh?"

"I promise," he said easily.

Jordan examined him skeptically. "I don't know. That sounded more like a politician's promise than an *actual* promise. Were you a Boy Scout?"

"I *was* a Boy Scout, actually."

"Then swear on your honor as a Scout." She jabbed her finger in his direction.

"I got kicked out of the pack." Ian grinned at her.

"Really? You must've done something pretty bad…."

"Not my finest hour," he admitted with a faint smile. "But I did belong to the Webelos, if that helps."

"What's a Webelo?"

Ian laughed. "Webelos. We be loyal Scouts."

"Are you in good standing with them?"

"As far as I know."

"Then swear on your honor as a Webelo that you won't laugh."

Ian held up three fingers of his right hand in a Boy Scout salute. "I swear."

Jordan eyeballed him contemplatively before she shrugged one shoulder. "Okay. I'll tell you. But only because you swore on your honor as a Webelo...and what's a little personal humiliation between friends, right? So—here goes." She took in a deep breath and then blew it out. "I used to have a huge crush on you."

"*Used* to? We just met. How could I have killed a crush that quickly?"

It took her a minute to catch his point. "No." Jordan shook her head. "I don't have a crush on you *now.* I mean that I had a crush on you when I was in *high school.*"

"Did we...*know* each other when you were in high school?" Ian asked her slowly, as if he was talking to an escapee from the loony bin.

"You don't have to look at me like that. I'm not certifiable. *No,* you didn't know me back in high school. But I knew you," she said. "Sort of."

"Meaning?"

"I had your Armani ad hanging on my wall." Jordan smiled sheepishly. "Framed."

"My Armani ad...?" Ian looked confused for a minute as he tried to figure out what she was talking about. Then he nodded. "Oh. You mean from my modeling days."

"Of course. What else?" Jordan looked at him curiously. She *felt* understandably embarrassed, but Ian was *acting* embarrassed.

"Wait a minute." She reached out and touched his sleeve. "I was supposed to be the one embarrassed. I didn't mean to embarrass you. *Did* I embarrass you? Or am I reading you wrong?"

Ian shifted uncomfortably. "No. You're not reading me wrong. I don't really like to talk about my modeling days."

"What? Why *not?* You were great at it!"

"I don't know how great I was at it," he said. "It was something I did so I could save up money to go to the Brooks Institute. Once I saved up enough money, I quit modeling and worked full-time on my bachelor's and then my master's in commercial photography."

"I get that. But why don't you like to talk about it? I would think that your past modeling experience would help you work with models now."

"It does. But because I'd been a model, it was a long time before the industry took me seriously as a photographer." Ian sipped his water. "I've always felt uncomfortable being the one in front of the camera. I'm much more at home behind it."

Jordan toyed with her straw. "It would never occur to me that someone who looks like you could feel uncomfortable in front of the camera."

He leaned against the bar and tucked one hand in his pocket. "I haven't always looked like this."

"You aren't going to tell me that you were an ugly duckling when you were a kid, are you?"

"Actually…I was," he said seriously. "In fact, I'll share something embarrassing from my childhood with you, so we're even. How's that?"

"I'm all ears." Jordan put her glass on the bar.

"When I was in middle school, I had buck teeth, acne…." Ian began to count out his adolescent flaws on his fingers. "I was shorter than all the girls in my class *and* I was overweight. My mom called it husky."

"I don't believe it."

"I'm telling you—it's the truth. And I remember the pinnacle of my middle school humiliation was when I asked five—" he held up his hand "—count them—*five* girls from my class to the seventh grade dance and not one of them accepted. I ended up staying home with my mom and renting a movie."

"It's really hard for me to believe you've ever had an awkward moment in your life. Much less get turned down by five girls. I bet they're all kicking themselves now!"

"Maybe." Ian shrugged. "But I've gotta tell you, being rejected that much during puberty can scar a guy." He pointed to his empty glass when the bartender checked on them. "I started running in middle school and the weight began to come off. By the time I got my braces off, I had grown about a foot and the girls at high school started to pay attention to me. But you know, the scar tissue never really goes away."

"I went stag to the prom because I towered over all the boys."

"We all come with our own share of baggage, don't we?"

"You're right. We all do."

Ian turned toward her. "So...wait a minute. Did you know I was the guy from the Armani ad the day we met on the street?"

Jordan pushed the hem of her dress toward her knees. "Uh-uh. Honestly...I really thought you were just another downtown wacko."

"Thanks," he said wryly.

Jordan continued. "To tell you the truth, when I look back on it, I *did* think that there was something familiar about you. But let's be real...it never occurred to me, not in a million years, that I would ever meet the guy in the

Armani ad. I'm a rancher's daughter from Montana and you're… Well. *You.*"

"And yet here we are. Together." Ian smiled quietly at her. "In paradise."

"I couldn't have imagined this if I tried." Jordan laughed. "You know what's funny? My sister's the one who recognized you. I'm the one who had your picture hanging up on my wall, but she realized that you were the guy in the ad. I've gotta be honest—I almost chickened out on the test shoot once I realized who you were."

"I'm glad you decided to show."

"Me, too." Jordan swiveled on her bar stool and nodded to the couple who had carved out the center of the dance floor to salsa. "One day I want to be able to dance like that."

After several moments of internal wrestling, Ian asked, "Would you like to dance with me, Jordan?"

She slid her eyes back to him. "Why am I not surprised that you can dance like that?"

"I'm a man of many hidden talents." He smiled at her.

She tilted her head. "Let me guess. You dated a professional dancer?"

"Dance instructor."

"You know…" Jordan swiveled her stool toward him. "It's amazing to me how much you have learned from all of these ex-girlfriends of yours. The only thing I ever learned from my ex was how to make a grilled-cheese sandwich with an iron."

"Would you like to dance with me, Jordan?" Ian repeated as he leaned toward her.

"Right now?"

"Can you think of a better place?" he asked. "We have this one free night in paradise. Why not take advantage of it? Unless, of course, I'd be stepping on someone's toes if we danced together. Then I would understand why you would say no."

"The only person stepping on anyone's toes in this scenario would be me stepping on yours." Jordan said. "I don't have a boyfriend, if that's what you're asking."

"It was." Ian's dimple appeared as he smiled at her. "So—we're both single. Can you think of one good reason why we shouldn't make the most of this night together?"

She felt slightly light-headed from the music and the night air and the insanity of Ian Sterling making a case for her to dance with him. It was like being transported to an alternate universe without any warning whatsoever. She was having a hard time wrapping her mind around it. And no matter how she tried to rework it in her mind, Ian was still her living, breathing fantasy man. The thought of being held in his arms—the thought of being pressed up against his body—made her feel excited, and slightly queasy with nerves.

"You know what?" Jordan decided to get over herself, throw caution to the wind and accept what might be a once-in-lifetime offer to dance with her fantasy prom date. "I do want to dance with you. As long as you don't mind my two left feet…."

"They'll go nicely with my two right feet," Ian countered, and she appreciated the fact that he was trying, as he always did, to make her more comfortable.

"But first, we've got to do something." Jordan wrinkled her nose at him.

"What's that?"

Jordan pointed to his jacket and tie. "You've gotta loosen up, GQ. This is Curaçao. You're *way* too uptight."

"You're an odd duck, aren't you?" Ian asked, smiling down at her.

"Quack, quack." She reached up and loosened the knot

in his tie. Once it was free, she slowly slid the tie out from underneath his shirt collar.

She put it on the bar and then held out her hand. "Jacket, please."

Ian smiled at her amusedly as he shrugged out of his jacket and passed it to her.

"Better?" he asked.

"Almost." She reached out, tugged on his right arm so she could unbutton his cuff and roll up his sleeve to just below his elbow. While he watched her with a bemused expression on his face, she performed the same action with his left sleeve.

"Are we good?" He held out his arms for her inspection.

Jordan pointed at his neck. "Undo the top two buttons and then we'll be good to go."

Ian quickly complied. "*Now* are you happy?"

She stood with her hands on her hips and gave him a head-to-toe once-over. With a nod, she said, "Yes. I am."

He held out his hand to her. "Shall we?"

Jordan slipped her hand into his and felt reassured as his fingers closed over hers. "This could turn out to be an absolute disaster."

"Relax, beautiful," he said near her ear. "I've got your back."

Ian had intended to dance only one dance with Jordan. But once he held her in his arms, once he experienced what it was like to have her body close to his, feel her vibrant energy radiating into his core, he wasn't in a hurry to let her go. Her brilliant blue eyes drew him in and held him captive. He wanted to breathe in the sweet floral scent of her skin again and again. But what he truly appreciated about Jordan, beyond the physical, was her spirit. Her laugh was infectious and her smile contagious. When he spent time with her, he felt lifted. He forgot about his diagnosis, forgot about his career. He forgot about all of it and just enjoyed the dance. For the first time in a long time, he felt like a normal guy spending time with a beautiful woman. And for him, that feeling was beyond priceless.

Jordan had hardly noticed as one by one the couples began to disappear from the dance floor. Ian had captured her attention while everyone else melted into the background. All her focus had been aimed at him. She concentrated on the feel of his tall, lean body as he guided her through the basic salsa steps. She absorbed the feel of his muscular arm beneath her fingertips and the strength of his hand on her back as he pulled her closer. He made it easy for her to relax and enjoy being swept up in his arms. And in his arms, she discovered an unexpected sense of belonging, an unexpected sense of security. She felt completely at home with Ian.

"Thank you and good night!" the band leader said into the microphone, marking the end of their last set for the evening.

Ian led her through one last turn and then they both stopped and clapped. Jordan looked around and realized that they were the only couple left on the dance floor.

"How long have we been out here?" she asked with a laugh. She felt hot and sweaty and *exhilarated*.

Ian glanced at his watch. "Right around two hours."

She pushed her hair back from her forehead and smiled up at him. "Now, that's how you spend a first night in Curaçao! Right? And I think I actually got pretty good there at the end. Don't ya think?"

"You held your own, there's no doubt about it." He walked her back toward the bar.

Ian collected his tie and jacket while Jordan grabbed a

napkin and wiped the sweat from her brow and neck. He smiled at her. Her face was flushed and glowing. Radiant.

"I suppose we should head back to our rooms," she said. She could hear the reluctance in her own voice. To be here, in Curaçao, with Ian, to have spent the night caught up in the embrace of a man whom she had dreamed about for years had been…*magical.* And she didn't want it to end.

"We're here to get a job done." Ian said this more as a reminder to himself than to her.

"You're right," she agreed. "I should force myself to get some rest."

"Shall we?" He gestured toward their rooms.

Jordan nodded and began to walk at a leisurely pace in the direction of the hotel. Ian fell in step and they walked together in silence. He reached to open the door for her, but missed it on the first try. She noticed, but chalked it up to his being tired as he found the handle and they walked through the door.

Once inside, she was met with a cold blast of air across her heated skin. She immediately crossed her arms over her body and began to rub her hands on her arms. Without a word, Ian draped his suit jacket over her shoulders. Surprised, she glanced up at him as her chilled skin was enveloped in his warmth.

"Better?" he asked as he pushed the up arrow for the elevator.

"Yes. Thank you. I really like that you're a gentleman, Ian." The jacket held Ian's scent and she had to squelch the urge to bring the material up to her nose and breathe in that unmistakable spicy, sexy cologne that was Ian's signature.

The elevator doors slid open and Ian waited for her to enter before he followed. His brow was furrowed and his mood had turned pensive. Neither spoke as they rode up to the third floor. She glanced at him as she stepped out into the hallway and saw that he was intending to see her to her door. She pulled the lapels of his jacket together, basking in the silken feel of the lining on her skin. When they reached her door, she slipped the jacket from her shoulders and handed it to him. She pulled her key out of her pocket, but hesitated to slide it into the lock. Ian stood beside her, jacket over his forearm, hands tucked into the front pockets of his pants. It seemed to Jordan that neither of them wanted the night to end, but they both knew it was time.

"Thank you for a great first night in Curaçao, Ian. For teaching me how to salsa." She swayed her hips slightly to emphasize the word. "I'll never forget it."

He briefly glanced up at the ceiling, as if to collect his thoughts, before he looked at her. The lighthearted Ian from the dance floor had given way to the quiet, introspective man who stood before her now. His smile had disappeared and the expression in his eyes grew intense as he responded.

"I had a great time with you, too, Jordan. You…helped me get out of my own head. It's been a really long time since I've given myself permission to have a little fun."

They both fell silent for several long seconds; neither one of them were in a hurry to say good-night. But the night had to end. And there simply was no other realistic ending to the evening other than for both of them to do so and go their separate ways.

She was about to take the initiative and step back when Ian cautiously reached out and gently brushed her bangs out of her eyes. Surprised, Jordan held her breath as his fingers traveled down the side of her face and under her chin. It was a soft, intimate touch.

"You're a beautiful woman, Jordan," he said in a low, gravelly voice as he pulled his hand away. "When I'm with you, you make me forget about everything that's…

bothering me." He slipped his hands back into his pockets to keep himself from pulling her into his arms. He wanted to kiss Jordan. He wanted to kiss her so badly. "I just wish that…we'd met at different time in my life—when things weren't so…complicated for me. When I didn't have to focus entirely on my career."

"Trust me, Ian. I get it," she said. "I've sworn off relationships myself until I finish the paintings for the show. But that doesn't mean that we can't be friends, does it?"

He found himself smiling again. "No. It doesn't."

Jordan unfolded her arms. "Can we hug it out, friend?"

Ian stepped forward, pulled her into his body and wrapped his arms around her. For a brief, exquisite moment, she was engulfed in the strength and warmth of his embrace. He held her so tightly that she could feel the steady beat of his heart. And in turn, she wrapped her arms around his waist and held him just as tightly as he was holding her. It was a moment between two people that was honest and tender, and it rocked her to her core. She had to force herself to slip out of his arms and take a step away.

Ian's face was in shadow, and she couldn't read the expression in his eyes as he moved back from her. She wished she could see his eyes clearly. Had he felt the electricity that had jumped between their bodies when they were pressed together?

"Good night, Jordan," he said solemnly.

She slipped her key into the door, waited for the green light to flash then turned the handle. "Good night, Ian."

He waited for her to step into her room and shut the door firmly behind her. As the lock clicked shut, Jordan leaned back against the door, closed her eyes and put her hand over her racing heart. After a moment, she picked up her phone and typed a text to her sister. She wrote simply, I think I fell in love 2nite and then hit Send.

And as she slipped into the cool, crisp, white sheets of her bed, Jordan replayed the events of the evening over and over in her mind. She never, for the rest of her life, wanted to forget this one incredible, romantic night that she had spent in the arms of Ian Sterling.

Chapter Eight

Ian didn't sleep well that night. After he dropped Jordan off at her room, he prowled around the penthouse, feeling unsettled and frustrated. Instead of reaching for the complimentary booze, he started knocking out crunches until the burn in his stomach muscles was too much to bear. Thoughts of Jordan whirled in his mind—her beautiful eyes, the softness of her skin, the sound of her laughter.

He had crossed a line with Jordan that he'd never crossed with a model on a shoot before, and he was angry that he couldn't even bring himself to regret it. He was crazy about her, that was the truth of it, and it had taken every ounce of his willpower not to kiss her good-night. The last thought he had before he drifted off to sleep was of Jordan, and he had awakened from a fitful sleep with the knowledge that she had invaded his dreams.

Unable to sleep, and unable to get thoughts of Jordan out of his mind, Ian decided the best cure for what ailed him was an early-morning run on the beach. He needed to sweat. Needed to expend some of his pent-up frustration. Needed to stop his preoccupation with Jordan and focus on the job at hand. He pulled on some running gear and grabbed his sunglasses before he headed down to the deserted beach. He knew this hotel like the back of his hand and that made it easier for him to navigate in spite of his reduced vision.

Once on the beach, he pulled off his tank top and dropped it on a lounge chair. He set out on his customary route, slowly at first, to let his muscles warm up. When the time was right, he sprinted along the deserted shoreline, reveling in the feel of the hard-packed sand beneath his feet and the burn of lactic acid as it shot through his thigh muscles. The constant stream of thoughts about the book, about the shoot, about his career, the future of his business, Jordan…were temporarily overridden by the sound of his heartbeat, his breath, and the crescendo of waves as they rolled toward shore. For the first time since he had landed in Curaçao, he felt the tension release from his back and shoulders.

Ian stopped at the far end of the private beach and stretched his hamstrings and calves. He stared at the cresting sun before he turned around and jogged back toward the hotel. He had a long couple days ahead of him—he needed to be laser focused on getting this job done. The fact that his eyes were a ticking time bomb was never far from his mind, and he knew he didn't have the luxury of wasting time. And this infatuation with Jordan—this *desire* for Jordan—needed to be controlled. But if he was being honest with himself, keeping his relationship with her platonic and professional was going to be a lot easier *thought* than done.

* * *

Before sunrise, Jordan awakened. She tried to fall back asleep, but was too excited about being in Curaçao to linger in bed. She quickly threw on a pair of cutoff denim shorts and a tank top, grabbed her sketch pad, some sunscreen and a towel and headed down to the beach. She sat down cross-legged on a lounge chair with her pad on her lap.

She could see the sun peeking out from the horizon and waited with impatient anticipation for her first Curaçao sunrise. As the rays began to bloom over the horizon, her attention was drawn to a lone figure jogging along the shoreline. She turned her head slightly to watch the man running along the beach. He was tall, broad shouldered and stripped bare to the waist. He jogged with an even, controlled stride of a seasoned athlete, and she found herself rudely staring at him as he approached. As he came closer still, it suddenly struck her that the man she had been admiring was Ian.

"Ian!" She called out to him and waved her hand in the air. She thought she'd seen him glance over at her, but he hadn't seemed to recognize her.

When he heard his name called by Jordan's familiar voice, Ian slowed his jog to a walk. In spite of his determination to resist his attraction to her, he had been thinking about her at the exact moment she'd called out his name. It was as if he had made her materialize with his thoughts. He turned toward the sound of her voice and started to walk over to where she was sitting. She had chosen a lounge chair that was located only a few feet away from where he had left his shirt.

"Hi!" she said again with another wave and a smile. She stood up and watched as he walked toward her with that confident natural swagger that reminded her of the first time she had ever seen him, on Sixth Street. Sweat glistened on his neck and arms and trickled down his torso onto his lean stomach. His hard, six-pack abs rippled as he caught his breath.

How could it be possible that Ian looked even better *without* clothing? It simply wasn't normal. He walked over to a nearby lounge chair and grabbed his shirt. He wiped his face off with it and then tossed it over his shoulder as he walked toward her.

Ian stood in front of her, hands resting on his hips, chest rising and falling from the exertion of his run. "You're up early," he said. "I thought you'd still be sleeping."

"No." She nodded toward the horizon. "I wanted to catch the sunrise. I figure I can sleep when I get home. What's your excuse?"

"I needed to get a jump on the day." He gazed at her bare arms with a frown. "Do you have sunscreen on? It doesn't look like you spend much time out in the sun."

Jordan glanced at her arms with a laugh. "This skin doesn't usually see much daylight, I've gotta admit. But I put sunscreen on. I just couldn't reach my back."

Ian held out his hand. "Here, let me have it and I'll get your back for you. I don't want you burned for the shoot."

She handed him the coconut-scented lotion and turned away from him.

"Sorry," he said apologetically as his hands glided across her skin. "I'm sweaty from my run."

"That's okay." She sighed as he began to rub the lotion onto her shoulders with his strong fingers. She actually liked the natural masculine scent of his body as it mingled with the fragrance of coconut. Even without his cologne, even with sweat clinging to his warm skin, Ian smelled good. She enjoyed the feel of his fingers as they glided across her back. It made her wonder what it would feel like to have him touch her in slightly more private places. But

Ian didn't linger on the task, and when he was finished, he quickly stepped away from her. He hadn't turned the event into a sexual innuendo, and yet the brief encounter had felt *intimate*.

"Thank you," Jordan said as she watched him wipe the residual lotion onto his torso.

"Not a problem." He walked over to the umbrella attached to her lounge chair and opened it. "We have to protect that beautiful skin of yours."

Ian slipped his tank top off his shoulder, shook it out and then slipped it on over his head.

"We're meeting in the hotel conference room today at noon," he told her. "The client will bring the merchandise, and then we'll get started."

Jordan's stomach lurched at the thought of actually having to model in front of a crowd. "Did it ever occur to you that you made a mistake bringing me here? What if I can't do this?"

"You can do it."

"How can you be so sure about that? You had to clear the studio just to get a good shot of me the other day. We aren't going to be alone this time."

"No," Ian agreed. "We're not. So you're going to have to block everyone out, Jordan."

"How do you propose I do that?" Her nerves made the question sound snappier than she had intended.

"You focus on me," he said in a calm, reassuring voice. "When you're in front of my camera, I should be your whole world. Remember that and you'll be fine," Ian declared confidently. "Listen. I've got to get going. Quit stressing about the shoot today. I've got your back."

"Okay." Jordan nodded. There was an assurance in his voice that she wanted to believe.

"I'll see you at the meeting…twelve sharp," he called over his shoulder as he headed back to the hotel.

Jordan sketched on the beach until the sun started to feel too hot. She packed up her stuff and then headed to the outdoor café to grab some breakfast. Then she went back to the room to get cleaned up for the meeting. Her roommate had arrived and was coming out of the bathroom when Jordan walked through the door.

"Hi, there. I was wondering when you were going to show up." The woman held out her hand. "I'm Ivory Wallace."

Jordan smiled at her. The model was six feet tall, rail thin, with milk-chocolate skin; she wore her inky-black curls in a freestyle afro. She had a toothy white smile and spoke with a heavy British accent.

"Jordan."

"Pleased to meet'cha. Where's home base for you?"

"San Diego. California."

"That's lucky. I'd like a nice, warm place to live," Ivory said as she flipped on an electric razor to dry shave her legs. "I live in Boston. Followed my boyfriend there. I can't stand it, though. Wicked cold in the winter."

"My brother and his wife live in Boston."

"It's nice if you don't mind freezing your butt off part of the year, I suppose. Not my cup of tea." Ivory dropped the razor on the dresser, then fished in her oversize Gucci bag and pulled out a bottle of lotion. "Did you arrive last night?"

"I flew in with Ian."

Ivory looked up from the task of putting lotion on her legs. "You're joking, of course."

Jordan shook her head. "No. We flew in yesterday. Why?"

"Ian *never* lets the models fly with him." Ivory snapped

the lid on her lotion bottle and tossed it into the bag. "I wouldn't go spreading that around, love. Jealousy is an ugly emotion."

Jordan's brow crinkled as she thought about what Ivory had just told her. It had never once occurred to her that Ian flying her to Curaçao on his jet was anything out of character for him. It made her wonder why he'd bent the rule for her.

"Thank God I got you as a roommate instead of one of the other two booked for this job. Total mean girls. You seem like a decent sort. Normal." Ivory leaned forward and checked her makeup in the mirror.

"How long have you been modeling?" Jordan asked as she riffled through her suitcase to find something suitable to wear for the meeting.

"For about five years now. It pays my tuition and keeps the lights on." Ivory sprayed her wrists with a vanilla-scented perfume. "God knows I can't count on my boyfriend to pay his share, the lazy baggage."

"Why don't you dump him, then?" Jordan asked.

"Now why would I go and do that?" Ivory slipped on a pair of sandals that complimented her Bohemian style maxidress. "He's a fantastic cook and he's great in bed." She slid on some chunky wooden bangles, then checked out her reflection before she turned to Jordan with her hands on her hips. "So. Are we going to this sodding meeting or what?"

After Jordan changed her clothes and freshened up, they headed downstairs. The crew that Ian had assembled was small but efficient; they were his personal team and they all knew how he liked his shoots managed. She recognized Violet Rios and one of models from his studio, but the rest were unfamiliar faces. Clint, Ian's assistant, was always strategically situated directly to his right.

During the meeting, Ian was focused, professional and direct. He laid out the plan for the shoot that would unfold over the next couple days. The Ian from the night before, the one who had held her in his arms and looked at her as if she was the only woman in the world, had disappeared.

Near the end of the meeting, the client arrived. Mrs. Lucca Vanderhoff, a young widow at forty-two, looked like a Brazilian version of Marilyn Monroe with her curvaceous figure, ruby-red lips, bronzed skin and long sable hair.

"Sweetness!" Lucca swept into the room, followed by a man who looked like a sumo wrestler squeezed into a navy blue pin-striped suit. "I'm so happy to see you!"

She air-kissed Ian on both sides of his face before he introduced her to everyone assembled.

"For Elite Jewelers this year, it's all about our fancy diamonds set in platinum." Lucca addressed the group enthusiastically. "We have *the* best selection of colored diamonds in the Caribbean and we have loyal customers from all over the world who depend on the quality of our diamonds and the craftsmanship of our custom designs. It is very important to *me* that this campaign is a reflection of our reputation and the Elite brand."

During her speech, Lucca stopped in front of Jordan. "Ian. I really like this new girl. With those eyes, I want her in the blue diamonds. But that hair is not for the Elite customer. You will be changing it, won't you?"

Jordan immediately bristled at the thought of this stranger demanding that she change her hair. *Her hair!*

Ian addressed Brando, his lead hairstylist. "Can you fix it?"

The man put his thumbs together and visually framed in her face with his hands. "I can fix anything, honey."

The meeting was adjourned and the crew quickly dispersed to get prepared for the first shoot. Jordan hung back and waited impatiently for several minutes while Lucca yapped about her new location.

"Excuse me." Jordan tried to interrupt the conversation as politely as she could. "Ian, I really need to talk to you."

"Can it wait?"

"No," she said with a shake of her head. "It really can't."

"She's feisty." Lucca smiled at her. "I like that.... Sweetness?" She turned back to Ian and again air-kissed his cheeks. "Take care of your girl. We'll have plenty of time to catch up later."

When Lucca was out of earshot, Jordan asked in a harsh whisper, "What was *that?* Don't you think you should consult with me about changing something that happens to be attached to my head?"

"No."

"No?" Her voice cracked on the question.

"No," Ian repeated impatiently. "The client wants it changed, so we change it. That's how this business works."

"But that's not how *I* work," Jordan said. "I don't want to change my hair, Ian. I have it this way because I *like it* this way."

He breathed in quickly and then blew out his breath with a frustrated sigh. "I don't really care whether or not you want to change your hair, Jordan. The only thing I care about *right now* is getting the shot and making this client happy."

Something in his tone made Jordan pause. She had known him for only a short time, but she could tell that something just wasn't right with him. On closer inspection, she saw that he appeared to be fatigued. Tense. Agitated. In fact, now that she looked back on the meeting, she realized that he had been squinting and rubbing his eyes the entire time.

Jordan forced herself to measure her words instead of just blurting out the first thing that popped into her brain. She felt tuned in to Ian's frequency in a way she had never felt with anyone other than her twin, and her gut was telling her that she needed to calm down and reconsider the situation. Honestly…did she *really* care about her hair, or was she just ticked off because she didn't like anyone dictating to her?

"All right," she said in resignation. "Have at it."

She could tell by Ian's expression that he was surprised she had given in so easily; he had obviously been bracing for a fight. He looked at her, really looked at her, for the first time this afternoon.

"Jordan." The intimate quality in his voice as he said her name struck a chord with her. "Your face and your eyes are the main event here, okay? It's not going to matter one way or the other what we do with your hair."

"If you say so," she said grudgingly.

His expression was serious as he asked, "Do you trust me?"

"Yes." Jordan looked up into his face. "Actually, I do."

"Good." He nodded. "Because I wouldn't let anyone touch your hair if I thought they were going to screw it up."

"All right." She nodded. After a short lull, she asked quietly, "Are you okay? You seem a little off to me."

"I'm fine. When I'm on a shoot, I'm just really focused on the task at hand. So don't take offense, all right?"

"Okay. I won't," Jordan said. One of the assistants poked her head in the door and waved at her. "It looks like they're ready for me."

"I'll see you on set." Ian slipped on his sunglasses. "And don't worry. You're in good hands with Brando."

* * *

"Embrace it and make it your own, honey." This was what Brando Kid, hairstylist and self-proclaimed diva, said to her as he finished precision-cutting her bangs.

Jordan leaned forward and studied her reflection. She now had a deep auburn pixie cut reminiscent of Twiggy in the 1960s. She had seen the look before on models featured in high-fashion magazines, but had never imagined having this type of cut herself. She reached up and touched her hair. "Uh…*wow*. That's crazy short."

"It's *flaw*less." Brando pursed his lips as he smoothed his pink-and-purple plaid silk shirt down over his bulky frame. "And don't get it twisted, okay? Let's not forget all that nastiness you had going on up in here." He swirled his finger over her head. "I had to strip you *all the way* down and then color you *all the way* back up. *Girl*...if it weren't for my God-given talent you could've ended up as bald as a baby's behind."

Ivory walked through the door of the room Ian had rented to prep the models and stopped behind Jordan's chair. She leaned over so Jordan could see her reflection next to her own.

"It's brilliant. You look like a proper model now."

"Amen and hallelujah." Brando snapped his fingers before he went back to cleaning his scissors.

Jordan shook her head slightly and ran her hand over her shorn hair. Her eyes looked huge compared to the rest of her features now. She looked weird. Almost alienlike.

"I suppose," she said to Ivory skeptically. "I wonder if redheads have more fun."

Ivory gave her a broad smile and put her hands on Jordan's shoulders. "Well, I hope for your sake that it's true. Ian's in rare form today—just a friendly warning."

Jordan didn't have much time to think about Ian's bad

mood. She was herded from Brando's chair to the next "phase" of her preparation. By the time she landed in wardrobe she had been tugged on, poked, prodded and pulled to the point that she thought she might just stand in the middle of the room and scream her fool head off. She was not a girlie girl like her sister, always in the mood for a mani-pedi; the last thing Jordan wanted was to have a bunch of annoying strangers fuss over her and primp her as if she was a pampered poodle on Rodeo Drive. Wardrobe dressed her in an overpriced designer one-piece bathing suit and she was then ushered out to the set, feeling more ridiculous and conspicuous than she ever had in her life.

Jordan walked out to the pool and felt her hollow stomach crumple inward. A large crowd of onlookers had gathered at the edge, and there were several hotel patrons watching the spectacle of the photo shoot from their balconies. She forced herself to lift her chin and square her shoulders in an attempt to hide her nerves. Her eyes swept the scene in front of her and located Ian. The moment she saw him, she felt a rush of relief. He was the safety float to which she would cling in order to keep herself from mentally drowning in fear.

When he spotted her, he waved her over to him.

"The hair works," he said. She could tell by the tension in his mouth and clipped way he was speaking that his mood had only deteriorated since the meeting.

Jordan self-consciously reached up and touched the hair on the back of her head. Before she could respond, Lucca and her sumo wrestler appeared with the briefcase.

"Open the case," the woman said to her companion as she inspected Jordan. "Delish!" she exclaimed with a smile. "The hair is a *million* times better. And now you have *two* eyebrows instead of one giant caterpillar crawling across your forehead!"

The sumo wrestler opened the briefcase and Jordan was immediately drawn to the one-of-a-kind, custom-crafted, diamond-encrusted jewelry held within. Large, heavy, exquisite pieces sparkled in the Caribbean sun; they had to be worth a fortune. Even though she was a tomboy to the core, when it came to jewelry, she was 100 percent female.

Lucca selected a two-carat, cushion-cut blue diamond surrounded by brilliant-cut white diamonds set in scrolled platinum. With a smile, she slipped the ring onto Jordan's finger. The shank was thick, but Jordan found that the weighty blue gem fit her as if it had been made with her in mind.

"A perfect fit, yes?" Lucca asked.

"Yes," Jordan responded, but didn't take her eyes off the piece. "This has to be the most beautiful ring I've ever seen. How much would something like this set me back?"

"This is a one-of-a-kind custom piece and it is a bargain at seventy-five thousand dollars."

Jordan laughed in disbelief. "Uh...*wow!* That's *crazy.*"

Lucca handed her a pair of matching earrings and said in a serious tone, "Not crazy if a man has the good sense to spoil the woman he loves."

Jordan smiled at the ring on her finger. "Well, then I obviously need to raise my standards, because I feel spoiled if someone takes me to the Old Spaghetti Factory for dinner."

"A woman should never allow herself to be spoiled so easily," the Brazilian replied with a cluck of her tongue.

Jordan raised her eyebrows. "Okay, you may have a point...but have you *tasted* their Garlic Mizithra? That cheese is to die for."

"No." She wrinkled her nose as if she had just smelled something bad.

"Well, let me just tell you, it's *incredible.* Pasta covered with Mizithra cheese, browned butter, garlic and sautéed mushrooms. If you ever find yourself in an Old Spaghetti Factory, you've gotta try it—I promise you it's worth the extra time on the treadmill."

Impatient to get started, Ian interrupted the conversation. "Are we gossiping or shooting?"

Lucca smiled up at Jordan as if they were confidantes. "Men. So easily frustrated."

Several people assisted Jordan into the pool so the top half of her body remained dry. Her hair and makeup were touched up. They took a couple test shots to check the lighting and then Ian was kneeling in front of her by the edge of the pool.

"Remember to focus on me and forget about everything else. Keep your face soft and the emotion in your eyes. You'll be fine."

It was obvious to her that she needed to play out a fantasy in her head in order to give him the emotion he wanted. So she decided to imagine that Ian was the man who had given her this ring, because that was a fantasy she could believe in. Seeing him today only confirmed her feelings from the night before—she loved him. She was *in love* with him. And as Ian picked up his camera and she trained her eyes on him, Jordan was surprised to discover that her nerves had melted away. This time it was easy to drown out the movement and the noise around her and focus all her attention, all her energy, on him. She did her best to emote with her eyes, and all she could do was hope that, when all was said and done, she wouldn't end up looking nauseous or nuts.

Chapter Nine

"Okay. Let's get started," Ian said as he crouched in front of her and pointed his camera. "That's nice, Jordan. I like that. Look to the left—chin up. That's it. Hold that. Now bring your hand up to your face so I can see the ring. Beautiful, Jordan. Just like that."

More than ever, he now had to rely on Clint's eyes at the monitor to make certain that he was getting the shot he wanted. Ian moved closer to the side of the pool and knelt down so he could frame a shot of the ring next to Jordan's face. The haircut had enhanced her delicate bone structure and made her high cheekbones and large almond-shaped eyes more prominent in her lovely face. When he saw her with the new style, his body had had the same visceral response reminiscent of the first time he had laid eyes on her. She was a stunning woman, but what made her even more alluring was the fact that she was unsure of her own appeal. Her insecurity and her awkwardness only elevated her beauty and added a layer of depth and fragility that intrigued him.

He had been having a lousy day before Jordan had reappeared. Right before they left for Curaçao, he had begun to notice a dark spot developing in his right central vision. Perhaps it was denial, but he had hoped that it was just an innocuous floater. But after his early morning run and a shower, Ian couldn't deny reality—he was starting to lose vision in his right eye now. And that was making him feel frustrated and anxious. Scared. When his right eye failed, the life he had built for himself would crumble. He would be disabled. He would be dependent. All day he had found it nearly impossible to focus on his work.

But when Jordan arrived, without being able to explain it, without really knowing why, he felt better. Grounded. Capable. In control again. And the minute he began to photograph her face, the minute he connected with the energy that was flowing from her body to his, the negative emotions drained out of him. And all that was left was the thrill of photographing Jordan.

He wanted to capture all that she was in one perfect shot. Her vivid blue eyes, as striking as the fiery blue diamond on her finger, were alive with intensity and emotion. She was telling a love story with the dreamy look on her face and her slightly parted lips, and he *believed* her. She broke through the barrier of the camera, reached through the lens and touched his soul. She was so sensual, so *provocative,* that he almost forgot himself. He almost forgot who he was, where he was and what he was doing. He almost put down his camera, pulled her out of the pool and into his arms.

"Gorgeous, Jordan." Ian encouraged her as he took several more photographs. "I like that right there."

Jordan didn't know how many photographs Ian had

taken of her by the time he stopped shooting and began to review her images on the monitor with Clint. After a minute, Ian nodded his head in the affirmative and Clint signaled to the crew that they were finished for the day. Jordan was greeted at the edge of the pool by Lucca and her sumo wrestler and was quickly divested of her jewels. Now wrapped in an oversize towel, she scanned the crowd for Ian. Her eyes darted from one person to the next, but she soon realized that he had left. A wave of disappointment swept over her. Perhaps it had been silly of her to want Ian to praise her when they were done. But she *had* wanted his approval. She had wanted his praise.

"Jordan…you were amazing!" Ivory had appeared at her side. "You looked like a seasoned pro out there."

Jordan forced herself to smile at her roommate, not wanting to let on that she was upset. Ivory was right. She had just accomplished something pretty major. She had forced herself to go through with her first public photo shoot and she had succeeded. She had prevailed. And with or without Ian's praise after the fact, she was proud of herself.

Ivory put her arm around Jordan's shoulders and they began to walk back to the prep area together. "The crew's getting together for a drink or two. Or four. Are you in?"

"Sure." Jordan felt as if she deserved to celebrate. "Why not?"

Jordan thought about Ian when she picked out a slim-fitting minidress to wear for the crew get-together at the bar. But when Ivory and she arrived there, Ian was nowhere in sight; Jordan felt so disappointed that she brought up it up to Ivory.

"You won't see Ian here tonight. Or any other night, for that matter," the model said. "I've worked with him on several jobs and he never hangs out with us. That's his deal. He doesn't socialize with the staff during the shoot and he doesn't shag the models. Bloody well smart of him if you ask me."

After drinking two virgin strawberry daiquiris and begging off several invitations to dance, Jordan was ready to leave. The main reason she had come to the get-together was to see Ian, and without him, the party soon lost its appeal. Now free of the crowd but not ready to return to her room, she slowly walked along an elevated boardwalk that separated the two private hotel beaches. The sound of a blues band playing in the bar situated at the end of the boardwalk serenaded her as she stopped and leaned against the wooden railing to admire the view. She breathed in the fragrant sea air and considered heading down for a quiet walk on the deserted beach below.

"If you're looking for the others, they're at the Schooner Bar."

The sound of Ian's voice reached her ears and she felt that familiar tingle in the pit of her stomach. She turned toward him. Dressed casually in jeans and a shirt that showcased his developed chest and toned arms, he walked toward her with a faint smile on his handsome face.

"No. I know," Jordan replied. "I just left there."

Ian positioned himself on her left side and leaned on the railing. "Why'd you leave? The night's still young."

She looked over at the beach before she answered. "It just wasn't for me, I suppose. I don't feel like drinking and I don't feel like dancing. So…"

"And the company?" Ian asked.

"Other than Ivory and Clint…I don't know." Jordan shrugged one shoulder. "I just don't have a lot in common with the rest of the crew."

"That was a PC answer if I've ever heard one." Ian

moved his arm closer to hers until she felt the warmth of his skin on hers.

"Okay, I'll confess. I admit that I wanted to punch Chantal right in the nose today when she said that she gave her dog away because it *outgrew* her purse."

Ian found himself smiling again. "Thank you for your restraint. I admit she's an unscrupulous dingbat, but she's a great model and I need her for the shoot tomorrow."

"You're welcome." Jordan leaned toward him and felt happy when he met her halfway and pressed his shoulder against hers.

Ian looked straight ahead, "You know...I wanted to tell you that I was really impressed with you today. You connected with the camera, you kept the emotion in your eyes and you gave me a lot to work with—different angles, really fluid movements. You've got a lot of raw talent as a model, Jordan. If you ever wanted a career in this industry, you could easily have one."

She glanced at his strong, masculine profile. "Thank you. I appreciate you saying that. I never realized how hard it was to model."

"You make it look easy," Ian said.

"Well, I'm just really glad that I didn't let either of us down."

"I never doubted you for a second," he assured her.

Whenever he was around Jordan, she managed to make him feel normal without even trying. It was hard to deny the positive effect she had on his psyche. He was glad that he had bumped into her. After the shoot, he'd retreated to the penthouse and closed all the blinds in an attempt to shut out the world. He had sat on the couch for hours, feeling sorry for himself as day gave way to night. But after a long time brooding in the dark, Ian realized that he had to drag himself out of the gutter or he wouldn't be able to function the next day. And regardless of his deteriorating eyesight, he still had a job to do. So he had forced himself to leave the room and head down to the beach in hopes that the fresh air and sea breeze would help clear his head. And then, as if by divine intervention, he had spotted Jordan alone on the boardwalk. It was if she'd been put in his path on purpose. As if she had been waiting just for him.

Ian turned slightly toward her. "So...you don't feel like drinking and you don't feel like dancing. What do you feel like doing?"

Kissing you.

That thought popped into her head instantly and she was glad that the words hadn't popped right out of her mouth. But it was the truth. She wanted to kiss Ian and be kissed by him. She wanted to be in his arms. She wanted the simple pleasure of holding his hand. She had given a pretty good speech the night before about being "just friends," but something inside her wanted a much deeper connection with Ian than that. She wanted to ignore the flashing warning signs. Bad timing or not, her heart was attaching itself to Ian.

"I was thinking about taking a walk on the beach, actually," she said, hoping that he would offer to join her.

"Do you want some company?" he asked quietly.

"Yes." Jordan's lips lifted into a small pleased smile. "I do."

They walked along the boardwalk together and, for Ian's sake, Jordan was glad that they didn't run into anyone from the crew. At the edge of the beach, he offered his hand so she could steady herself as she slipped off her shoes. Barefoot, she stepped onto the sand and then sighed with pleasure. It was cool and slid between her toes as she wiggled them.

"You have to take off your shoes, too." She pointed to his feet.

"Are you always this bossy?"

"That's the pot calling the kettle black!" Jordan exclaimed as she hooked the straps of her shoes onto her fingers and crossed her arms. "Come on. Make it snappy, GQ."

Ian stared at her for several seconds before he shook his head, kicked off his shoes and then pulled off his socks.

"Happy now?"

"Ecstatic," she said playfully as she dug her toes into the sand. "Now...doesn't that feel good?"

"No."

"You're such a grouch, Ian. Really and truly you are."

Jordan smiled up at him with a look of sheer pleasure on her face and Ian couldn't help but smile back. She had managed to lift his spirits in no time flat. And the more he thought about her, the more he realized that he wanted to make room for her in his life. After all, he had already made room for her in his heart.

"Why do I like you so much, Jordan?" he asked.

"I have no idea. But I'm glad that you do." She took a step forward with a wave of her hand. "Come on. Let's go."

They walked side by side toward the shoreline and they both stood still as the water raced up to their feet and lapped over their ankles.

"It's so beautiful here," she said as she held out her arms and twirled around in the moonlight. "I love this hotel, don't you? The history of it."

"That's what keeps me coming back," Ian said as he began to walk farther down the beach. "This place has been here since the late 1700s. First as a Dutch colonial mansion and then as a residence for the governor of Curaçao. Now it's a hotel. After all this time, it's still here."

"It had to reinvent itself so it could survive."

"Sometimes you have to adapt or die, I suppose," he mused, briefly remembering the conversation he'd had with Dylan about restructuring their business.

"Most people are afraid of change because they think that what they have is permanent. It's not, though. The only thing consistent about life *is* change."

As they walked slowly toward the tall rock breakwaters at the end of the private beach, Ian reached out for her hand.

Surprised, Jordan looked over at him.

"Is this okay?" Ian asked. He held her hand loosely enough that she could easily pull away. Instead, she slipped her fingers more firmly into his and tightened her hold.

Hand in hand, they walked quietly together. Jordan hadn't expected this private, stolen moment with Ian. But it was a fantasy come true and it felt as if the planets had aligned just for her.

When they reached the cool, jagged gray rocks of the breakwater, Ian said, "This beach is too short."

She laughed softly. "We should talk to management about that."

"First thing," he agreed, not letting go. "I'm not ready to go back."

"Neither am I." Ian's hand was a perfect fit for hers.

He looked around. They were in a completely private part of the beach—secluded. Free from prying eyes.

"Any objection to hanging out here?" he asked.

"No." Jordan lowered herself onto the softly packed, dry sand. "I'm from Montana, remember. I'm not afraid of a little sand."

She patted the spot next to her. "Take a load off, GQ. We have the best seat in the house here."

Ian sat down next to her, bent his legs and wrapped his

arms around his knees. For a moment they were quiet, soaking in the ambience of the deserted beach. There was a warm breeze rolling in with the waves as they crashed onto shore. The bright, full moon cast a golden-yellow hue across the darkened blue water of the Caribbean.

"This is exactly what I needed." Jordan sighed as her arm brushed against his.

"I was just thinking the same thing," Ian said quietly. "I can shut off my brain out here."

"You're right." She rubbed her hands down the length of her bare legs and dug her toes into the cooler layer of beach sand.

"So…did you hear from your mom?"

Jordan groaned and shook her head. "Oh, my God, *yes*. I finally had to just shut off my phone—between the calls and the emails and the text messages, my bill next month is going to be outrageous. Thank God the woman isn't on Twitter!"

Ian laughed. "Well, I hope she has a forgiving nature. I don't want to burn my bridges with her before I get a chance to work my charm on her face-to-face."

"*You* don't have to worry about my mom—*you* she will love. Trust me. And don't worry, Mom doesn't hold a grudge. She has a very specific method of working through things that bother her. First, she freaks out. Then she rearranges the kitchen. After she rearranges the kitchen, she bakes something fabulous, which totally makes my dad happy because he has a serious sweet tooth. And then she gets over it."

Jordan smiled and tipped her head back as the night air curled around her upper arms and bare throat. "I could stay here all night. Do you know that? I could fall asleep right in this spot. Curaçao is one of the most beautiful things I've ever seen."

Ian looked over at her. He felt fortunate in that moment that Stargardt hadn't robbed him of his night vision yet. He was able to make out the long, slender curve of Jordan's neck and the lovely profile of her face.

"I think you're one of the most beautiful things *I've* ever seen," he said to her.

Jordan bumped his shoulder with hers. "If you don't stop saying things like that to me, you may never be able to get rid of me. And then you'll be sorry. I'm just sayin'."

"Why do you always make a joke when I try to say something even remotely serious to you?" Ian asked.

"Because," she answered.

"Because why?"

"I don't know—maybe because it seems really crazy to me that I'm sitting here *in Curaçao* with the guy I used to have hanging on my wall…."

"I wish you'd stop looking at me as that guy in the ad and start thinking of me as the man who's sitting beside you right now," he said, and there was a subtle thread of frustration woven into his words.

"I'm trying," Jordan said defensively. "But it's not just that, Ian. I feel like there may be something *developing* between us, and I promised myself I'd take a break from relationships and concentrate on my art. It might not seem like it to you, but I get my heart broken really easily and the last thing I need right now, with a deadline looming, is another broken heart."

"I've had my heart broken, too, Jordan," he said quietly, openly. "Every serious relationship I've ever been in, I've been in it for love. I've always wanted what my parents had. A great marriage. A family. True love. And so far it just hasn't worked out for me like that. But even though we both have a lot on our plates, I can't stop myself from wanting to take a chance with you…." He skimmed his thumb over her slender knuckles. "You know…my father felt that he was in the right place at the right time to meet my mother. And now I feel like I've been put in the right place to meet you. I don't want to ignore what I'm feeling for you just because the timing is off."

Ian heard his words coming out of his mouth and felt slightly detached from them. In fact, he couldn't believe his own ears. His heart seemed to be overriding his brain and had temporarily taken control of his vocal cords. The last thing he had expected to do this evening, in the middle of shooting for the Elite campaign, was to be making a case to Jordan to start a relationship. But sometimes things just couldn't be planned for in life. And all Ian knew was that he had been feeling lousy when he had come down from the penthouse and now, being in Jordan's company, he felt better. She made him feel better just by being there with him.

When she didn't respond immediately, he asked, "How do you feel about what I just said, Jordan?"

She looked down and shook her head almost imperceptibly. "I'm not really sure *how* I should feel. I mean, last night, we both agreed that starting a relationship right now doesn't make sense…."

Ian dug his fingers into his shin as he waited for her to continue. Had he put his heart on the line for nothing?

"But I have to be honest, Ian. I'm crazy about you. It feels like I've known you for years instead of just days. And even though there's a part of me that still thinks we shouldn't jump into this right now, the other part of me just wants to be with you."

He turned his face toward her. "Which part of you is going to win?"

"The part that wants to take a chance on whatever this

is between us." Jordan leaned her body into his. "Hands down."

Ian let go of her hand and put his arm around her shoulders. With his other hand, he reached up and gently turned her head toward him. He leaned in and touched his lips to hers. His lips were firm and soft as he lightly kissed her. His warm hand moved to the back of her neck as he deepened the kiss, tasted the inside of her mouth.

Jordan made a noise of pleasure in the back of her throat as he slipped his hand under her knees and lifted her onto his lap. His heavily muscled arm became her support as he wrapped her tightly in his arms and devoured her mouth with his. Jordan pressed her body into his and matched Ian's passionate kisses with passionate kisses of her own. His fingertips traveled down her throat, grazed her breast, before he gripped her hip and rocked her into his hardening groin. She felt an explosion of tingling at the apex of her thighs, felt her heart beating wildly in her chest.

Ian pressed a trail of kisses along her neck as he stroked the skin of her bare legs from the top of her thigh to her ankle. Jordan closed her eyes and tilted back her head as his palm slowly traveled back up her leg to the hem of her dress. His fingers pushed the material upward, his fingertips gently stroking the skin just beneath the hem. Jordan breathed in, her lips parted, when he kissed her exposed throat.

Ian's fingers left her naked thigh and traveled upward to her breast. His large hand covered her small breast and she could feel the heat of his skin through the thin material of her dress. Her nipple hardened as she pressed herself into his hand. Her heartbeat was drumming in her ears as she splayed her own hand over Ian's chest.

"Ian," she said in a breathy voice. "I think we need to slow down."

"You're right," Ian whispered huskily in her ear as his hand moved from her breast back up to her face. "This isn't where I want us to make love for the first time."

Jordan pressed her face into his neck and said with a self-effacing laugh, "I've been observing a self-imposed celibacy. If we had gone much further, I was afraid I wouldn't have been able to stop…."

He hugged her tightly and dropped a kiss on the top of her head. "I'm just crazy about you, Jordan. Do you know that? Whenever I'm with you, I forget about everything except how good it feels to be near you…."

She moved off his lap but held on to his hand. "I think I'll take that as a compliment…?"

"I meant it as a compliment." He smiled at her in the moonlight. "I haven't been able to let my guard down around someone in a really long time."

"I like that," Jordan said, as she wrapped her arms around her body. The night air had cooled while they were caught up in each other's arms.

Ian noticed her shivering. "Cold?"

"A little."

"I suppose we should head back anyway." He stood up. "We have a busy couple days ahead of us."

Jordan accepted his hand as he helped her to her feet.

"I just hope that things calm down south of the border by the time we reach the boardwalk," he said as he adjusted himself inside his jeans.

Jordan smiled as she watched him trying to make his erection less noticeable. "Picture the most unsexy thing you can think of—like your friend's grandmother in lingerie—and you'll be back to decent in no time at all."

"Okay—that was a *horrible* image you just put into my head!"

"Well…" She picked up her shoes and dusted off the bottom of her dress. "Did it work?"

Ian bent down to retrieve his shoes, then reached out for her hand as they headed back to the boardwalk. "Like a charm." He laughed. "Problem solved."

"See?" She pointed her finger at him. "I told you so. It works every time."

Ian and Jordan walked slowly toward the lights of the hotel. As they drew closer to the sounds of the jazz band and the voices of the hotel patrons, she let go of his hand, but he pulled her back into his arms.

"This's a strange situation for me," he said, his lips hovering above hers. "I don't usually get involved when I'm working on location."

"Ian…" Jordan lifted up on her tiptoes. "Just shut up and kiss me."

After they shared a final kiss, she walked back to the hotel as if she was floating on air. She was in love. It was official now. And the most amazing, shocking development of all: Ian Sterling—hunky, handsome, Adonis Ian Sterling—was wild about her, too. She was so excited that she wanted to scream it, text it or tweet it to all her friends and family. But a promise was a promise. For now, it would have to be a secret—a wonderful, incredible, *crazy* secret.

Chapter Ten

After two more days of shooting, Ian announced that they had gotten all the shots he needed for the campaign. Ivory and Jordan returned to the room to pack up their belongings and get themselves ready for the wrap party. Jordan hurriedly scooped up all her clothes out of the drawers and tossed them into the open suitcase on her bed.

"Anxious to get down to the pub and see Ian, are we?" Ivory asked her.

Jordan tried to hide her surprise as she glanced at her roommate. "I'm excited to see everyone…including Ian."

"Oh, *please!*" Ivory exclaimed. She waved her hand in the air. "There was so much sexual tension flying around between you and Ian during the photo shoots, it actually made me miss my boyfriend! The two of you should just get a room already—which shouldn't be too bloody difficult, since you already *have* rooms at this hotel."

Jordan's brow wrinkled. "It's that obvious?"

"Totally obvious." Ivory zipped up her suitcase. "But it made for a great show, I can tell you that much."

They finished packing, took turns in the bathroom and then headed down to the bar. Jordan couldn't wait to see Ian. They had managed to steal a couple private moments together since their first kiss on the beach, and he liked to send her flirtatious texts. Jordan loved all her stolen moments with Ian, but her favorite was when they'd found themselves alone on the elevator and Ian had pinned her up against the wall and kissed her all the way to the third floor. But the moments had been far and few between, and Jordan had her hopes up that they would be able to steal away from the group on their last night together in Curaçao.

"Sex on the Beach times two, barkeep!" Ivory had cleared a path for them all the way to the bar. After she ordered their drinks, she surveyed the crowd, looking for the rest of the crew. "Hey, there's part of our·clan over there."

They grabbed their drinks and headed to the other side of the dance floor. Halfway there, Jordan spotted Ian, Lucca and Clint sharing a table. Lucca was hanging on Clint like a Christmas-tree ornament, while Ian seemed to be a world away in thought. The minute he spotted her, he left the table and walked directly to her side.

"I've been waiting for you," he said without an ounce of pretense. "Do you want to get out of here?"

Ivory gave her a conspiratorial wink. "All I can say is it's about time." She sucked down her Sex on the Beach, put the glass on a nearby table and then relieved Jordan of her drink. "I'll watch this for you. You kids run along now and have a good time."

Jordan smiled at her roommate. "Don't wait up."

"I wouldn't dream of it," Ivory replied, before she

headed to the table where the rest of the crew had parked themselves.

Ian put his hand possessively on the small of Jordan's back and walked closely behind her as they skirted the perimeter of the dance floor. The minute they made it through the crowd, he reached for her hand.

Jordan beamed at him as they moved away from the noise of the bar. "I've missed you."

"I've missed you, too," he said with a smile that showed off his dimple. "All I've been able to think about for the past couple days is getting you alone."

"Where are we going?"

Ian opened a side door to the hotel. "My room."

Jordan's stomach flip-flopped as she walked through.

He led her over to the elevator and pushed the up arrow. "Is that okay?"

"You read my mind…."

The minute the doors to the elevator slid shut, Ian leaned back against the wall and pulled her toward him. She pressed herself into the full length of his body as she dragged her fingers down his corded back.

"You smell good enough to eat," he said as he kissed the side of her neck.

"Do you think anyone else from the crew noticed us leaving together?" she asked with a breathy sigh.

Ian captured her face between his large hands. "Beautiful, I don't care if they saw us or not. The job is done, I'm free, and I intend to spend my last night in Curaçao doing exactly what I want to do."

"I was just thinking of you," Jordan said as the doors to the elevator slid open.

He grabbed her hand and brought it up to his lips. "I know. And I love you for looking out for me. But I don't want to worry about anything right now. I just want to spend time with you."

Jordan followed him to the penthouse, keenly aware that he had used the *L* word. Was that just a turn of phrase, or did he really mean that he *loved* her?

Inside the penthouse now, he fixed drinks for them and then they headed out to the balcony. Jordan sat down on the two-person chaise and scooted over so Ian had enough room to join her. She leaned back against the plush cushion and soaked in the Curaçao sounds and smells. She would miss the feel of the warm, misty Caribbean breeze on her skin and the faint smell of flowers in the air. She would miss the sound of calypso music that set the perfect backdrop for the island's laid-back vibe.

Instead of sitting beside her, Ian sat down on the edge of the chaise and faced her.

"Why are you all the way over there?" she asked as she put her glass down on the floor beside her.

Ian looked out at the horizon pensively before he brought his eyes back to her. He reached for her hand and held it in his. "I need to talk to you about something."

Jordan's gut immediately tightened before she could force it to relax. "That's never a good way to start off a conversation…."

"I know," he said. "But there's something you need to know before…we go any further."

Ian's words caught her attention and she pushed herself into a more upright position. Her entire body stiffened with nervous anticipation.

"You're not about to tell me something horrible, like you're addicted to *Duck Dynasty*…are you?" Jordan tried to break the tension by making a joke.

"No," he said with a smile in his voice. "Nothing as horrible as that."

She pretended to wipe sweat from her brow. "Well, that's a load off."

After several seconds of silence, Ian asked in a more serious tone, "Did you know that I was engaged?"

Jordan was glad that her face was in shadow and he couldn't see the guilty look that was surely plastered there. She had searched Ian on the internet after their test shoot together and had run across hundreds of pictures of Ian with his ex-fiancée.

"Actually, yes. I did know about that," she admitted. "I've seen pictures on the internet. She's really pretty."

"We've never really talked about our past relationships...." Ian said.

Jordan shrugged one shoulder. "I don't really like to talk about mine. They're in the *past* for a reason. I'd rather keep them there."

"And I can appreciate that. In fact, I respect that about you. But I think it's important that you know why my last engagement failed."

"All right...." Jordan said cautiously.

Ian could feel his heartbeat speed up at the thought of telling Jordan about his condition. He hadn't been able to sleep the past two nights just thinking about how to handle this subject with her. He knew himself well enough to know that he had fallen hard for Jordan. She was on his mind nearly every minute of the day. He missed her when she wasn't around, and he couldn't wait until he could be back by her side.

This wasn't a fleeting infatuation. He had fallen in love with Jordan Brand. He wanted to take a chance with her, try to build a life with her, but before they could move forward, he needed to tell her about his eyesight. And he knew it was a risk. She was so young, so carefree. He had no idea how she would react to the news. But as nervous as he was that Jordan would reject him, he knew that the moment to tell her was now.

Quietly, he said, "A few months after I asked Alexia to marry me, I was diagnosed with something called Stargardt disease, and she ended up calling off the engagement."

The minute Jordan had heard the word *diagnosed,* she'd pushed herself away from the cushion to sit upright and listen more closely. This wasn't what she had anticipated *at all.* She had thought, instinctively, that she was going to hear a tale of infidelity.

She gripped Ian's fingers a little more tightly as he continued, "Stargardt is a rare form of macular degeneration—"

"My grandfather had MD," Jordan interjected as she tried to process what Ian was saying to her. "But he was eighty-nine. You're so young...."

"Stargardt is a juvenile form of macular degeneration," Ian explained. "Most people with it go blind in their teens. But some people are diagnosed later in life—like me."

Jordan's heart seized when she heard the word *blind.* She had watched helplessly as her grandfather's world had slowly faded to black as MD stole his eyesight.

"Ian...." She put her other hand on his arm to show her support. "I'm so sorry. I'm sure you've already gotten a second opinion...?"

"And a third." He nodded. "The diagnosis stands."

"Is Stargardt the same as wet macular degeneration? Honestly, I've never heard of it before...."

"I wish *I'd* never heard of it," Ian said bitterly. He stood up and walked over to the balcony. There, he put his back to the railing and crossed his arms over his chest. "But to answer your question—it's different. Basically, I'm losing my central vision in both of my eyes. The progression of

Stargardt is so different for everyone who has it that the doctors can't tell me how long it will take for the disease to progress—or how far it will go. But chances are I'll be legally blind in both eyes. I'll still have my peripheral vision, but…"

His words trailed off and they both remained silent as the minutes ticked by. Jordan needed a moment to digest what Ian had just told her. She thought of her favorite grandpa and all the problems he'd had with his vision loss before he passed away. Her mind naturally started to review her time with Ian, trying to identify those little idiosyncrasies that had never really made sense…until now.

"Do you understand what I'm saying to you?" Ian's question broke into her internal dialogue.

"Yes, Ian. I understand."

He braced himself for rejection. She was so quiet, it was hard to gauge how she was going to respond. "And how do you feel about it?"

"How do I feel…?" Jordan repeated the question as if she hadn't understood it. "I feel…horrible about it. I mean, I'm stunned. I'm not sure what else *to* say, other than I'm sorry. I saw how hard it was for my grandpa, and I just can't believe that it's happening to you. You're so young."

"I meant—how do you feel about getting involved now that you know this about me?"

"Oh," she said, surprised. She patted the spot next to her on the chaise. "Ian—can you come over here and sit next to me? You're too far away."

He sat down to her left. "I can see you better out of my right eye."

Jordan turned her body toward him and linked her arm through his. "Then I'll always make sure I'm on your right side."

With her free hand, she covered his fingers with hers. "This must've been really hard for you to tell me...."

He nodded. "I've been really worried about how you'd react." There was an emotional undertone resonating in his voice that touched her heart. "But I couldn't let things get more...serious between us without you knowing what's going on with me."

"Because you thought that...maybe I wouldn't want to be with you because of this?"

"It's happened before."

Jordan shook his arm a little bit. "But it's not happening *now*. Ian, listen to me. I appreciate you telling me about what's going on with your eyes so I can help you, but this doesn't change how I *feel* about you." He had opened himself up to her, had rendered himself vulnerable before her. She wanted to reciprocate, level the playing field and put her own skin in the game. She reached up and lovingly touched his face. "If you haven't figured it out by now, Ian—I'm in love with you. And I want to be with you no matter what."

Ian didn't respond verbally to her profession of love. Instead, he gathered her up in his arms and kissed her with a renewed hunger—a renewed passion. Jordan wrapped her arms around his waist; it didn't take long for her body to start buzzing with excitement. Ever since the passionate moment on the beach, her libido had been kicked into overdrive. She felt as if she would die from sheer sexual frustration if Ian didn't make love to her as soon as possible. She needed to feel the weight of his body on top of her. She needed to feel him inside her. Making love to Ian wasn't something she just wanted—it was something her body *needed*.

"Do you want to go inside?" he asked as his fingertips skimmed the curve of her breast.

Jordan arched into his hand. "Yes."

Ian took her hand in his and led her through the living room into the bedroom. Once there, she pulled his shirt out from the waistband of his jeans and began to unbutton it. Ian stood quietly, watching her intently, as she unbuttoned the last button and slipped his shirt off his shoulders. She tossed it onto a nearby chair.

"I've been dying to do this ever since I saw you jogging on the beach," she said as she ran her hands down his bare chest. Her fingers lightly circled his nipples before they traced the ripples in his abs as she made her way down to his belt.

"Your body is a work of art, Ian." Jordan unbuckled his belt and slipped it out of the loops. The belt landed on the chair next to his shirt. "You're the reason artisans in ancient Greece chiseled statues out of marble."

Jordan went to unbutton his jeans, but he stopped her. She looked up into his handsome face. "Don't you want to make love to me, Ian?"

He brought her hand up to his lips. "You know I do."

"But…?"

"But I want to make sure that you understand—if we make love…that means we've decided to be together."

Jordan wrinkled her brow as she thought. After a moment, she half smiled and half laughed. "Are you saying that I can't use you for your body?"

"I think that's what I'm saying—yes." He seemed a little surprised by his own words.

"Ian, I haven't been intimate with anyone for over a year now. If I didn't think that I had a chance of making this work between us, we'd still be down at the bar. Fair enough?"

"Fair enough," he said as he reached out and pulled her

thin white T-shirt over her head. He tossed it on the chair with his shirt and belt.

"You're so beautiful, Jordan," he murmured as he easily unhooked her bra and was able to see her small, perfectly formed breasts for the first time. "So sexy."

Jordan peeled off her jeans down to her bikini briefs and watched as he stripped down to his snug-fitting, leave-nothing-to-the-imagination boxer briefs. Her eyes were immediately drawn to the large bulge straining against the inseam.

"Oh!" Something popped into her mind. "Hold that thought. Don't go anywhere!"

She ran into the living room, grabbed something from her wallet purse and then returned the bedroom. When she arrived, Ian had pulled back the covers and was sprawled out on the bed, completely nude.

Jordan stopped in her tracks and took a moment to admire his body. Her eyes drifted from his powerful thighs up to his hard, erect shaft.

"I bought these yesterday, just in case." She held up a package of condoms. "Good thing I got the magnums."

"Come here," Ian said in that sexy, suggestive baritone voice of his that sent a shiver of anticipation shooting through her body.

Jordan dropped the box of condoms on the nightstand, and snuggled herself into Ian's side. Pressed tightly against him, Jordan closed her eyes and gave herself over to Ian as he explored her body with his hands and his lips. She felt his fingertips travel down her stomach and beneath the waistband of her underwear.

She started to squirm, and made frustrated noises in the back of her throat. It had been such a long time since she had been in someone's arms that her body accelerated from zero to one hundred miles per hour without much encouragement. She bit the side of Ian's neck as his warm fingers slipped between her thighs.

"Oh, my God, Jordan," he said in a strained, rough voice as he felt her for the first time. "You're so ready for me."

The minute Ian's fingers found her, Jordan pressed down into the heated skin of his hand, asking for more—asking for a release from a frustration that had been building in her for months. She cried out as an orgasmic wave rushed through her body. As the ripples of sensation began to ebb, she rested her head on his chest and held on to his shoulder. Her breathing was rapid and shallow and she felt embarrassed that she had climaxed so quickly.

Ian looked down at her. "Did you just have an orgasm?"

"Yes." She breathlessly bent her head and kissed the swell of his chest. "I told you it's been a long time for me…."

He tipped up her chin. "Do you want another?"

"Yes." Jordan reached down between them so she could wrap her fingers around his hard shaft. "But do you think that we can skip the foreplay and just go straight to the lovemaking part? I really need to feel you inside me."

Caught off guard by the request, he studied her for a second before he responded, "I can do that."

Jordan slipped out of her panties as Ian slipped on a condom. They met back in each other's arms in the middle of the bed. She reached for him eagerly as he lowered himself onto her. Jordan opened her body and reveled in the weight of him as he pressed into her.

Ian's moans mingled with hers as he buried himself inside her. "You feel so good to me, Jordan," he groaned against her lips.

She wrapped her legs around his flanks and held on tight while Ian loved her. He loved her slowly. He loved her deeply. He loved her as she had never been loved before. Every stroke, every movement, every kiss felt as if he was writing a love song to her with every sensual move he made. He worshipped her with his body as she caught wave after orgasmic wave. Exhausted and satiated at last, she dragged her fingernails down his back as he surged into her one last time. He cried out her name as his entire body tensed and then shuddered with his own orgasm.

Ian rested his full weight on her for a moment before he propped himself up with his arms. He leaned down and kissed her gently.

"That was incredible," he said as he rolled onto his back and brought her along with him. He tucked her protectively into his side as he let out a contented sigh. "*You* are incredible." He dropped a kiss on her damp forehead.

Jordan laughed softly as she rested her face on his chest and her hand over his heart. "You are, too."

They both fell silent, feeling languid and spent. Jordan let her fingers slide over his skin, which was slick with perspiration; she felt his heartbeat start to slow beneath her fingertips.

"Jordan?" Ian said her name so sweetly.

"Hmm?"

"I love you." It was a quiet, simple confession from a man used to keeping his feelings close to his chest. "I think I must've loved you the minute I saw you on the street that day, but I just didn't know it. I thought that I was just looking for a model for my book…but now I know I chased you down that day because I felt something for you the very first time I saw you."

Jordan had become very still in Ian's arms. When she didn't respond, he asked, "Do you believe in love at first sight?"

She propped herself up on her elbow so she could look down into Ian's perfect, chiseled face. "Yes, I do…because it happened to me with you. I fell in love with your image all those years ago, Ian, when I was a teenager. And now I've fallen in love with you all over again, but this time with the man, not the image."

Ian must have been happy with her answer, because he wrapped his arms around her and rolled her onto her back. He was aroused and wasn't shy about letting her feel it.

"Again?" she asked, surprised.

"Beautiful." He wrapped his arms tightly around her and kissed her hard on the mouth. "Prepare yourself for a very long night."

Chapter Eleven

Jordan had spent her last night in Curaçao tangled up in Ian's arms. They slept in late, made love and then ordered room service. After they finished breakfast, she went back to her room to pack the rest of her toiletries. Ivory had sent her a text early in the morning to say goodbye, and when Jordan returned to the room, it was strange not to have her friend's energy and stuff sprawled out everywhere. After one last, forlorn look around, Jordan met Ian downstairs and they headed to the airport.

Once back in San Diego, they both returned to their separate lives, throwing themselves into their individual projects. Ian finalized the dates and locations for all the San Diego locations he wanted to feature in his book, while Jordan searched for a loft with the right light and enough space to set up her easels and paints. With the extra she'd made modeling in Curaçao, plus the advance she'd received for Ian's book, she had given her notice at

Altitude so she could dedicate herself full-time to painting. Although they kept in touch through phone calls and texts, they hadn't seen each since they had returned to California. So when Ian asked her to accompany him to a friend's barbecue, she accepted his invitation with a mixture of excitement and nervous anticipation.

He picked her up in his car outside her condo, and right before she slid into the backseat of the Bentley, she couldn't stop herself from wondering: What if the magic between them in Curaçao hadn't followed them to San Diego? But the moment she got into the car, Ian answered her question by pulling her into his arms and kissing her long and hard.

"Hi." She laughed when he let her come up for air.

"Hi, beautiful." He draped his arm around her shoulders. "I've missed you. Any luck with the studio hunt?"

"*No*. If I can afford it, the neighborhood is way too shifty."

"I was afraid of that." Ian nodded his head. "Listen— I've been thinking about something and I want to run it by you."

She shifted her body so she could look at him more easily. "What is it?"

"Well, I have this unused space upstairs in the studio. It's small, but it's got a large window and natural light. And I was thinking—why don't I just clear out that space and let you set up your easels there?"

Jordan tilted her head curiously and lifted her eyebrows. "You want me to work in your studio?"

Ian put his hand on her leg. "Yeah. I do. What do you think about that idea?"

It took her a few seconds to formulate her thoughts into words. "I mean—I think it'd be great. I could stop looking for a space and use that time to paint. But—wouldn't I be cramping your style?"

Ian sneaked in a quick kiss onto her lips before he responded. "Honestly, I've spent way too much time this past week thinking about you when I should've been working. I think I just might get *more* work done if I have you nearby."

Jordan stared at him for a while, astonished. And here she had been worried that he hadn't missed her at all.

"So what do you think?" he asked her. "Do you want to move in with me?"

Jordan felt a sudden surge of relief and excitement flood her body. She flung her arms around his shoulders and rained a dozen little kisses on his tanned cheek.

"Is that a yes?" he said with a laugh. Holding Jordan in his arms was what he'd been missing all week.

"Are you kidding?" Jordan hugged him more tightly. "That's a *heck* yeah!"

As the car approached Dylan Axel's Mission Beach home, Ian started to have second thoughts about his decision to attend the party.

He shook his head slightly as he looked out at the condo. "I usually avoid this type of situation. There're too many new faces, too many people to keep track of…."

Jordan reached out for his hand and squeezed his fingers. "Yeah, but I'm here now. We're gonna have a great time together. I promise."

On the sidewalk, Jordan got her first real look at Dylan's three-story condo.

"Uh…*wow!* This is a-maz-ing."

Ian smiled as he offered his arm to her. "He bought this to impress the ladies, and it looks like he succeeded. It's a bit like musical beds in there on the weekends. I stopped playing those games a while ago."

"Well, I won't hold it against him." Jordan slipped her fingers into the crook of Ian's arm.

They walked up to the entrance of the condo and Dylan—tall, athletic and charming—greeted them at the door.

"I don't believe it! You actually came!" Dylan wore a broad smile on his face. His features weren't as chiseled or striking as Ian's, but he was a good-looking, confident man with a spectacular surfer's build.

"And you brought a date! Will wonders never cease?" He held out his hand to Jordan. "I'm Dylan."

"Jordan." She smiled up at him.

"Come in! Welcome to my humble abode." Dylan took a step back so they could walk through the door.

His condo on the inside was sexy and sleek, and just like Dylan, didn't seem to take itself too seriously. From the wide-planked wood floors to the bamboo cabinets and the floor-to-ceiling windows that showed off the spectacular beach views, the condo was designed for a bachelor looking for a good time. Jordan could tell, right off the bat, that Dylan's main goal in life *was* to have a good time—and she liked him immediately.

"We'd better get him a drink before he backs out," Dylan said to Jordan. Dylan fixed Ian his usual and handed his friend a glass. "You know I want you to slow down the drinking, but I think tonight calls for an exception."

Dylan fixed Jordan a whiskey sour and then gave them a quick tour of the condo. He had just led them out onto a large balcony overlooking the beach when a tall, athletic blonde parted the crowd and headed straight to Dylan's side.

The newcomer linked arms with Dylan. "Brianna wants a picture of us for her blog."

"Jenna, you remember Ian," Dylan said.

"Hey, Ian," Jenna said with a nonchalant air.

"And this is Ian's girlfriend, Jordan," Dylan continued.

Jenna looked Jordan over. "You're gorgeous. Do you model, too?"

"Only for Ian." Jordan smiled up at Ian.

Jenna tugged on Dylan's arm and started to walk backward. "Come on. Brianna has another party to go to. You can talk to Ian anytime."

"I'll be back," Dylan said sheepishly as he followed his girlfriend down the stairs to the lower deck.

Even though Ian couldn't always see the people surrounding him, they spotted him. For the next hour, he was inundated by friends and acquaintances that hadn't seen him out in months. Jordan felt overwhelmed by the constant bombardment of people vying for Ian's attention; she could only imagine how he was feeling. He appeared to be perfectly calm on the outside, but his arm encircling her waist was stiff with tension.

"How are you doing?" Jordan asked Ian quietly when they had a moment alone.

"I'm ready to get out of here," Ian said testily.

"We can't leave yet. We haven't been here long enough. Why don't we go down to the fire pit and get some fresh air?"

After a moment of thought, Ian nodded. "I'm going to hit the restroom first. I'll meet you down there."

"You'll be okay?" she asked.

"Don't worry. I know this place like the back of my hand."

"Okay. I'll be waiting for you." Jordan lifted her chin so he could kiss her lightly on the lips.

Jordan walked down the stairs to the fire pit and found seating for two. Her head was buzzing with the names and faces of the people she had just met. It hit her that she needed a break from it all nearly as much as Ian did.

She breathed in the salty sea air and looked past the quiet beach to the crashing waves. She was drifting off into her own thoughts when a voice at her side startled her.

"Hi," Dylan said as he sat down next to her. "I'm glad I caught you alone. I don't know how you did it, but it's amazing that you got Ian to come tonight. I can't remember the last time he was here. It's gotta be years."

"He asked me," Jordan said, not wanting to take credit for something she hadn't done.

"Yeah, but he came because he wanted to show you off."

"I'm glad that we could make it," she said with a small smile.

"Me, too. But, again—amazing." Dylan leaned his forearms on his legs. "Ian told me that you know about what's going on with his eyes."

She nodded. "He told me when we were in Curaçao."

"Well, he must think you're pretty special, because he doesn't share that bit of news with anyone. So I was thinking, if you can get him to do something like this—coming to this party—maybe you can get him to do something else that he really needs to do…."

"Like what?"

"Go to the doctor," Dylan said firmly. "He needs to go see his specialist. He's supposed to be getting regular checkups, and he's been acting like if he just ignores this thing, it'll go away." Ian's friend lifted his hands in a show of frustration. "I've tried to get him to go, but he won't listen to me. Maybe he'll listen to you…."

"Hey! Are you trying to steal my girl already?" Ian asked as he walked down the stairs toward them.

They both turned their heads and looked up at him.

Dylan stood and gave his friend a quick male version of a hug. "You can't blame a guy for trying, can you?"

"No," Ian said as he held out his hand to Jordan. "But she's meant for me."

After a long walk on the beach, Ian insisted on heading home. Jordan said goodbye to Dylan, and she could tell by the parting look he gave her that he was hopeful she could get Ian to take better care of himself—to manage the disease more carefully. Arm in arm, they headed back to the car. The chauffeur was awaiting their return and opened the door for them. Back in the car now, nestled comfortably in Ian's arms, Jordan decided to wait until another moment to mention Dylan's concerns. This was her first night in San Diego with Ian, and she didn't want to spoil it by bringing up issues that could ruin their good time.

"I'm not ready for this night to end," he said as he rested his chin lightly on top of her head.

"Neither am I."

"I'd like to take you home with me." There was a gruff, sexy quality to Ian's voice and Jordan knew that his mind had turned to lovemaking ever since their passionate embrace on the beach.

"Okay." She snuggled more deeply into his body. He was so solid and strong and smelled so spicy and masculine. She couldn't wait to strip down and feel his naked skin against hers once again.

When they reached downtown San Diego, the driver turned into the underground parking garage of one of the two highest high-rises. Jordan swiveled her head around. "This is Harbor Club Towers. You live *here?*"

"Yes."

"We're neighbors!" Jordan exclaimed, surprised. "I live just two blocks north of here."

"I know," Ian said cryptically.

"Why so secretive?"

"I like my privacy. No one bothers me here."

"That's because no one actually knows that you live here!"

He smiled as he pulled her back into his arms. "Exactly."

They took the elevator all the way up to Ian's two-story penthouse. When he opened the heavily carved, ornate door, Jordan felt as if she had been immediately transported into another world.

"*Wow!* This looks like something right out of *Town and Country* mag." She pointed to a large empty spot in the entrance. "That's the perfect place for a painting. You could put one in that alcove with some down lighting."

When they reached the second-floor landing, Ian asked, "Do you like it?"

At the top of the grand staircase, Jordan was met with an unfettered view of the city and San Diego Bay. The view was spectacular, but the decor seemed way too ornate and fussy to be Ian's taste.

"The view is amazing," she said, trying to highlight the positives.

"But...?"

"But...the decor is a little too..."

"French country revival gone wrong?"

She laughed. "You took the words right out of my mouth."

Ian shrugged out his jacket and laid it across the back of one of the plush, overstuffed couches that faced a curved wall crafted entirely from floor-to-ceiling glass panels.

"I bought it for the views. It came furnished, and one day, when I've got the time, I'll change it."

"It's easy to overlook the furniture with a view like

that," Jordan agreed. "I bet they're even more incredible during the day."

Ian pulled out the cork from a wine bottle, felt for the edge of a glass and then replaced his fingers with the lip of the bottle. He poured them each a glass of sweet red wine. "You'll be able to see for yourself in the morning," he said as he held out her glass to her. He lifted his own glass and let her touch her rim to his. "Cheers."

Jordan hadn't been sure if he intended for her to stay overnight, but now that he had said as much, she felt herself relax as she sipped on her wine. She wanted to stay with Ian overnight. In fact, she wanted to stay with him more than she should.

"Let's go out onto the balcony." He walked toward one of the French doors facing the bay. "I want you to see the view from outside."

Jordan walked outside, felt the cool breeze on her face, heard the city sounds drifting up from the streets far below and felt as if she was standing on top of the world. They were higher than anyone else in the city and the uninterrupted views stretched before them for miles.

"It's incredible, Ian. I've never seen anything like it," she said when she reached the balcony railing.

Ian walked up behind her and wrapped his arms around her waist. She leaned her head back against his shoulder.

"And now you know how I felt the first time I saw you…." He kissed the side of her neck.

Jordan shivered. She wasn't certain if it was from the cool night air or the feel of Ian's lips on her skin. She turned in his arms and found his lips with hers.

"Take me to bed," she whispered. "I've been away from you for too long."

Wordlessly, Ian took her glass from her fingers and placed it on a nearby table. He returned to her side and then swept her up into his arms. Jordan wrapped her arms around his neck as he carried her to the master bedroom, where she stretched out across the bed and waited for him to join her. He quickly stripped out of his clothes and then made short work of her top, jeans, panties and bra.

She reached for him, but Ian held back. This time, he wanted to take his time; he wanted to drive Jordan wild before he brought their bodies together.

She willingly relinquished control to him as he loved her body all over with his fingers and his lips and his tongue. When he finally gathered her up in his arms and pressed his flesh into hers, she felt as if her body was on fire. He took her to the edge of ecstasy again and again only to pull back and leave her aching for more.

"I'm so in love with you, Jordan," he said as he slowly, thankfully, joined their bodies together.

Jordan gasped when he buried himself deep inside her. She called out his name as an intense orgasm exploded through the core of her being. Ian held her tightly as the orgasm ebbed, and then he began to take her on another climb, another journey, toward another peak. She felt his love for her with every touch and every kiss and every thrust of his hips as he rocked into her body. Jordan wrapped her arms and legs tightly around him as his thick muscles began to tense and tighten.

Ian crushed her in his arms and buried his face in her neck as his body shuddered with his own intense orgasm. Jordan hugged him tightly to her and laughed unbelievingly at the lovemaking she had just experienced.

"I love you, Ian." She kissed his cheek and tasted the salt from his perspiration on her lips. "So very much."

He rolled onto his side, as he always did, and took her with him so she was still in his arms. "I love you, too, beautiful."

Jordan curled her body around his and closed her eyes. Never in her wildest dreams had she imagined that she would love and be loved by someone as wonderful as Ian Sterling. But this *was* her life. It wasn't a dream. And in that moment, she felt incredibly lucky, incredibly blessed.

"Jordan?"

"Hmm?"

"Could you imagine yourself living here?"

Her eyes popped open and she lifted herself up slightly so she could look at his face. "It's not exactly the kind of home I've ever pictured for myself."

"What if you had free rein to change it so it *did* feel like home to you?"

"What are you saying, Ian? That you want me to move in with you?"

"Maybe not tomorrow, or even next week, but... eventually. Yes. And I was just wondering if this is a place you could learn to love...."

"Ian, I'm so crazy about you I'd live with you in a cardboard box."

"Let's hope we can always do a little bit better than a cardboard box." Ian's arms tightened around her. "And you'll stay with me tonight—so you can see the views in the morning?"

She put her head back down on his chest. "Yes. I'll stay with you tonight. And if you have all the ingredients, I'll cook my world-famous French toast for you."

"How are you at late-night cooking?" Ian asked.

She propped herself up on her elbow. "Are you hungry?"

"Famished."

Jordan sat all the way up and scooted to the edge of the bed. "Well, then, come on—get up, GQ. Let's go see what you've got in that gourmet kitchen of yours."

* * *

Jordan cooked up some omelets with the hodgepodge of ingredients Ian had in his cabinets, and then they ate and drank wine and talked late into the night. In the morning, after one of the best sleeps she'd ever had in California, she awakened to an empty bed. She slipped on one of Ian's button-down shirts before she hunted him down in the home gym.

"Good morning." She smiled at him.

"Nice outfit." He smiled at her.

Jordan performed a curtsy. *"Gracias, señor."*

Ian slowed the treadmill to walking speed and grinned at her. He was wearing his sunglasses, protecting his eyes from the bright morning light pouring through the giant windows.

"I'll be done in a minute. I made coffee," he said as he started to increase the speed again.

"My hero. Meet me out on the balcony when you're done." Jordan blew him a kiss before she headed back to the kitchen. She poured herself a mug of coffee, went out onto the balcony and sank down into a comfortable lounge chair. The view was even more spectacular during the day. The sun was shining brightly in the cloudless, turquoise-blue sky and it felt warm as it touched her skin, but not too hot. It was perfect.

Ian soon joined her, sweaty and sexy in a tank top and workout shorts. He sat down in a chair next to hers and put his feet up on the coffee table.

"Now how do you like the view?" he asked as he wiped the sweat off his face and neck with a towel.

"Ridiculously amazing." She held her hand over her eyes to shield them from the sun. "Well worth the sleepover."

He smiled at her suggestively. "I hope a few other things made the sleepover worthwhile."

Jordan returned his smile, but it faded slightly as she looked from him to the beautiful penthouse views. A depressing thought reverberated in her brain: not only was Ian on the brink of losing photography, which was his life's passion, but he was slowly, incrementally, losing these views he had worked so hard to attain. It made the undercurrent of frustrated energy that emanated from him more understandable.

"Ian?" Jordan put her coffee cup down and straightened her spine.

"Hmm?"

"I wanted to talk to you about something and I guess now is as good a time as any...."

"What's up?" He rested his arm across the back of the chair.

"Well, ever since you told me that you have Stargardt, I've been trying to educate myself about it...researching it online."

"Okay."

"And a lot of the sites say that people with Stargardt disease need to see a doctor who specializes in low vision for regular checkups...."

Ian brought his arm down off the back of the couch. "Dylan talked to you...."

"Yes," she said plainly. "He did. He's worried about you. But so am I. And if you haven't seen a doctor recently, then I want you to go."

Ian leaned forward, rested his elbows on his thighs and rubbed his hands over his shorn hair several times. He blew out his breath before he looked over at Jordan. He hadn't known her all that long, but he did know her well enough to suspect that she wasn't going to let up until she got her way.

"I don't like to go to the doctor, Jordan. All they do is dole out lousy news."

"I understand that, Ian. And I even understand you not wanting to go. But we need to know what's going on with your eyes. I mean—have you noticed any changes since the last time you had a checkup? Have you consulted with someone who sells low-vision products? I remember everything we had to do with my grandpa. There's a lot that needs to be managed here...."

Ian stood up and walked over to the edge of the balcony. There was part of him that wanted to tell Jordan to mind her own business, to let him handle it in his own way, in his own time. But he knew she was right. And he knew that his right eye had taken a turn for the worse while he was in Curaçao; he just didn't know how much of a turn. Perhaps it was time to find out.

He leaned back against the railing and crossed his arms on his chest. "If I set up the appointment, will you go with me?"

Jordan's heart skipped a beat as she nodded. "Of course."

He crossed over to her, bent down, tilted her chin up with his finger so he could kiss her on the lips. "All right," he agreed. "I'll set it up later. But in the meantime, do you want to join me in the shower?"

"You mean in that shower built for ten?" Jordan accepted Ian's extended hand. "Lead the way, GQ."

Chapter Twelve

The next two weeks flew by for Jordan. As good as his word, Ian had the space upstairs cleared out, and she moved all her painting gear there. And once she was settled in, she threw herself into her first piece. When she wasn't painting, she was on set with Ian, modeling for his book. He wanted to feature all his favorite San Diego spots in it. They'd already had a photo shoot at Petco Park and the San Diego Zoo. And over the next few weeks he had planned photo shoots at Balboa Park, as well as the floating navel museum, the USS *Midway*. Whether they were working or playing, they had become an inseparable pair. They were permanent fixtures in each other's lives, and Ian insisted that his crew treat Jordan with respect. Even Violet, who hadn't been one of her fans from day one, was cordial. And Jordan's twin, Josephine, had also given Ian the stamp of approval. So at the moment, it seemed as if their relationship was totally on track.

Jordan looked at her watch to check the time and then put down her paintbrush. She washed her hands, freshened up and headed downstairs to get Ian.

She poked her head around the room divider. "Are you ready?"

He was leaning toward the computer screen and squinting through his reading glasses at the most recent images he had captured for the book.

"Is it time already?" he asked. She could hear the beginning resistance in his voice.

"Yep," Jordan said. "Come on. I don't want to be late."

"Maybe we should go another day. I'm right in the middle of something here."

She walked over to his computer and turned off the monitor. "We're going."

Ian sighed audibly as he stood up. "Why don't we call them and see if we can set up an appointment for next month…?"

Jordan stepped behind him and pushed on the small of his back. "No. This doctor is booked for *months*. We're just lucky that someone canceled and you got the appointment. So you're going. David's downstairs with the car, so let's boogie."

Ian was agitated and irritable all the way to the doctor's office, but Jordan refused to let it sway her from the task at hand. They both needed to know how far the disease had progressed; it was just too important to be put on the back burner. Once there, he signed in and handed the receptionist his insurance card, driver's license and the stack of papers they had downloaded from the doctor's website.

"This is a waste of time," Ian said gruffly as he put his license back in his wallet and sat down next to Jordan. "I have a ton of stuff that I needed to get done *today*."

"Name one thing that is more important than this?" she asked him a loud whisper.

He glanced at her and repeated, "This is a waste of time."

"Well, I don't think it is. And Dylan doesn't think so, either...."

Jordan felt completely calm and in control the entire time they were in the waiting room, but the minute they were called back by the nurse, she broke out into a whole-body flop sweat. Ian sat down in the exam chair while she perched herself on the edge of the chair by the door. For both their sakes, she was glad that it didn't take long for the doctor to knock on the door. A slender, high-octane man in his late thirties entered the room.

"Ian, it's nice to see you again!" Dr. Harlow shook his hand. "It's been a long time."

Ian nodded at Jordan. "Jordan convinced me it was time to come in and get checked out."

"I'm glad she did. I'm glad she did." Dr. Harlow shook her hand before he sat down on a rolling stool. "It's important for folks to get their eyes checked every year, but it's even more important for anyone who's been diagnosed with any type of macular degeneration to come on in for regular checkups." He looked back and forth between them as he spoke. "So let's get down to brass tacks—how have things been going with your eyes? What concerns do you have, and what changes have you noticed?"

"My left eye seems like it's a lot worse. If I close my right eye, most of what I should be able to see directly in front of me—" Ian pointed to where Jordan was sitting "—is really blurry. I know Jordan is sitting there, but I can only see her shoes and the lower part of her legs."

"How's your peripheral vision working for you?"

"Lately, I've had to rely on it more than I'd like to with

my left eye," Ian said. "But the thing that's really been bothering me is this new blind spot in my right eye. I'm a professional photographer and if my right eye goes—" he shook his head "—I don't know how I'll be able to work."

"I can understand your concern. When did you first notice this change in your right eye?" the doctor asked as he input notes on the laptop.

"A little over a month ago."

"All right...." Dr. Harlow nodded. "Any signs of night blindness?"

"No. Not yet," Ian said. "Just extreme sensitivity to bright light."

"And," Jordan interjected, "I've noticed that Ian has a lot of trouble with depth perception. He'll reach for something and either miss it or knock it over...."

Dr. Harlow spun the stool toward her. "That's because we need both eyes to be able to perceive depth, and right now, Ian's left eye isn't pulling its share of the load. Make sense?"

"Yes." She nodded.

"Okay." Dr. Harlow stood up. "So I want to give you a thorough exam today. I'd like to dilate your eyes...."

"I'd rather not do that." Ian shook his head. "I have a lot of work to do and I don't want my eyes to be all screwed up for the rest of the day. More than they already are."

"I completely understand your reticence," he said. "But the drops I have will only keep you dilated for ten, fifteen minutes tops. I want to see how your eyes are functioning with visual acuity, color acuity and field, but I'd also like to take some images of your retina so we can check any changes in the macula compared to the baseline images we took on your last visit, and unfortunately, that requires dilation."

"You need to do it," Jordan said quietly.

Ian looked at her for several seconds before he finally agreed.

"Good. Good." Dr. Harlow moved an arm of one of the machines in front of Ian's face. "Let's get started, then. Just put your chin in the cup, press your forehead forward and look straight ahead. These machines are so advanced now, it changes how we do business around here. It's all computerized and digitalized."

He consulted a laptop nearby and looked at the numbers the machine had generated from testing Ian's eyes. He then moved another machine in front of Ian. After making several adjustments and asking him a series of questions, he moved the machine back.

"Okay," the doctor said. "There have been some significant changes in the visual acuity of the left eye. When I last saw you, you were 20/40 corrected in the left eye. Now you're 20/100 corrected in the left eye and 20/40 corrected in the right eye."

"So—not legally blind yet," Ian stated.

"No. Not yet."

"And you can't tell me when that might happen…."

Dr. Harlow shook his head. "No. It could be two weeks, it could be two years."

"It feels like things are getting worse more quickly now," Ian said in a flat voice.

"I would have to agree with you, Ian." The specialist nodded as he stood up and grabbed a small bottle of drops. "Let's get your eyes dilated so I can take a closer look at them."

Ian tilted back his head while Dr. Harlow inserted the drops. He handed him a tissue to wipe his eyes, then brought up yet another machine as he rolled his chair closer to look into Ian's eyes with a light.

"All right," he said, looking at the back of Ian's eyes. "I

do see some new damage in the macula in the right eye as well as the left." He paused. "I'm going to capture some images of your retina now." Dr. Harlow took pictures of Ian's eyes and the images popped up on the screen.

Jordan stood up and walked over to Ian. She took his hand in hers. "How are you doing?" she asked, as the doctor looked at the results.

"Not bad compared to what it's normally like to have my eyes dilated," Ian said.

"You'll be back to normal by the time you leave the office," Dr. Harlow assured him, moving to the side so Jordan and Ian could see the laptop screen. "Let's take a look at your images. Do you see this right here—these yellow-and-white spots?" He pointed. "That is the current scope of the damage to the macula in the right eye—which is causing the blind spot you were concerned about."

Jordan glanced over at Ian nervously. He sat perfectly still, eyes squinted, reading glasses on, as he stared at the enlarged images of the macula in both eyes.

"I'm sorry…. Dr. Harlow, would you mind explaining to me what's causing the damage? I'm still not sure I understand." She narrowed her eyes so she could focus more intently on the images.

"Stargardt has been traced back to a mutation in two different genes, depending on the form, which can be determined by genetic testing…."

"I have autosomal recessive," Ian told her.

"I thought I saw in your chart that you'd had the testing. So this means that Ian has a mutation in a gene called ABCA4," the doctor explained. "The mutation in this gene causes light-sensitive cells in the retina's macula to degenerate. The macula is in the very center of the retina… right here." He pointed to the screen. "This is where the most sensitive vision is concentrated. When the macula is damaged, as it is with Stargardt, visual acuity is reduced, visual sharpness is reduced and the ability to see color is often impaired, as well."

"And there isn't a cure for this—some sort of treatment we could start?" Jordan could hear the tension in her own voice as her stomach twisted. She had heard some of this from Ian, but somehow, coming from Dr. Harlow, it all seemed so *permanent*.

"Not yet." The doctor switched on the light in the small room. "What we can do right now is try to slow down the progression of the disease and help you adapt to the loss of your central vision. We need to protect the eyes from UV light—and you have several options available to you other than sunglasses. You could be fitted with tinted contact lenses with specialized melanin filters that would help with any sensitivity you may experience with glare and bright light. Some people find this more convenient than taking sunglasses on and off. We also have photochromic glasses that turn dark when they are exposed to light— again, some find this more convenient that taking sunglasses on and off all day…."

"That would help." Jordan nodded.

"Make sure you wear a wide-brimmed hat when you're outdoors, and limit your alcohol intake, as well as foods rich in vitamin A. I'm writing you a new prescription for your reading glasses." Dr. Harlow looked at Ian. "And I'm going to refer you to an equipment specialist who can help you identify any low-vision aids that might help you continue to live a full and independent life. We can also provide you with the contact information of the local support groups."

Dr. Harlow wrote out the prescription and then clipped his pen back onto his pocket. "The most important thing, Ian, is for you to believe that you can still have a fulfilling life. Stargardt will make things more challenging, but it doesn't have to be a dead end for you. Individuals with this condition have careers and hobbies and relationships… but—" Dr. Harlow glanced at Jordan and paused before he continued "—I would recommend, if you are considering starting a family, that you seek genetic counseling."

"I'm going to get a vasectomy," Ian said flatly with a quick shake of his head. "I'm not going to pass this on to anyone else."

Jordan did her best to keep her expression neutral when Ian mentioned a vasectomy; this was the first time she had ever heard him mention it. And they had jumped into their relationship so quickly that they hadn't had much time to discuss marriage and children. It had never occurred to her that Ian's diagnosis would stand in the way of them having a family together. She had always imagined herself with a large family, surrounded by children and a truckload of grandchildren. She was born to be a mother.

"Everyone has to decide what's best for them, Ian, and if that's what you eventually decide, we can refer you to some doctors who handle that procedure. In the meantime, I'd like to see you again in four weeks." Dr. Harlow handed Ian his prescription. "Plan on being here for several hours so we can get some additional testing done—map out the exact size and location of the blind spot in the right eye."

Jordan shook Dr. Harlow's hand and smiled at him. "We'll be here."

"Good. Good." Dr. Harlow smiled back as he opened the door. "I'll see both of you then."

They walked out of the doctor's office in a somber, reflective mood. Emotionally, Jordan was transported back to the time in her life when her beloved grandfather had been first diagnosed with macular degeneration. All those feelings of pain and helplessness and uncertainty flooded her body, and it was just occurring to her that she had fallen in love with a man who shared a similar fate as her grandpa. Once Grandpa Brand had completely lost his vision, he had never been the same. She had watched his enthusiasm and zest for life drain away as his eyesight failed him. And now Dr. Harlow's words had left an indelible mark in her mind. Like her beloved grandfather, Ian *was* losing his eyesight—she had seen the pictures firsthand. The disease was real and it appeared to be progressing rapidly. Perhaps she had been living in her own state of denial, because Ian was so young and so talented and so *perfect*. It seemed implausible to her, a blow against the natural order of things, that he should be going blind.

Jordan glanced over at Ian as the Bentley pulled out onto the road. He was leaning against the door, looking out the window, understandably pensive and closed off. She put her hand in the space between them, offering it to him if he wanted to hold on to her for support. But for the entire ride back to the studio, his hand remained balled up in a fist on his thigh. When they reached the studio, there were no words spoken between them as they took the elevator up to the third floor—and there were no words between them as they walked into the quiet, darkened loft. Jordan closed the door behind her and leaned back against it. She felt nauseous from stress and sadness and uncertainty; she wasn't sure what to say or what to do. In a way, she wished she had never insisted that he go the doctor. What had it really accomplished, other than to make Ian feel worse?

She pushed away from the door and walked slowly over to where he was pouring himself a drink. Her first instinct was to stop him from downing yet another tumbler of Scotch, but she managed to squash the thought before she verbalized it. Ian poured himself a second drink, downed it, before he slammed the empty crystal tumbler onto the marble counter. Jordan jumped slightly at the sound of crystal hitting stone, and was relieved when the glass didn't break in his hand. The pain, the rage, the frustration that Ian was feeling was etched deeply into the handsome lines of his face. She wanted to reach out to him, try to comfort him, but she couldn't bring herself to cross the invisible barrier he had erected between them the moment they'd left Dr. Harlow's office.

Ian slumped into his favorite spot on the couch and dropped his head into his hands. Jordan followed and perched next to him. She didn't try to touch him, but wanted him to know she was there for him if he needed her. She could only imagine what he was going through right now; it was one thing to *suspect* that things had gotten worse and quite another for it to be confirmed by a specialist. Denial was a powerful tool, and she had no doubt that this visit with Dr. Harlow had forced Ian to abandon some of the denial that had been helping him function in his daily life.

Tentatively, Jordan reached out and put her hand lightly on Ian's leg. He didn't pull away, but didn't reach for her, either.

"Why are you still here?" she heard him ask her in a strained voice.

"I love you." Jordan's response was immediate. "Where else would I be?"

He pressed the heels of his hands over his eyes and rubbed away the tears seeping onto his lower lashes. He glanced over at her, his eyes reddened with brimming emotion.

"Why would you want to be with someone who *has* this?" he asked her angrily. "Everything I am right now—a photographer, a businessman, a *whole* man—is going to disappear! Don't you *get* that? I'm going to be washed up before I'm thirty-five!"

"That's not true. I don't believe that, not for one second, Ian. There's so much help out there now, so much technology...."

"What kind of *help* is going to save my career when I'm *legally blind,* Jordan?"

He pushed her hand off his leg, but she refused to move from her spot on the couch. Ian's anger was normal, even expected, and she was certain it would pass—eventually. And she sensed that it was important for her to prove to him that he could depend on her, that she wouldn't bail at the first sign of trouble.

"I don't know the answer to that, Ian, but I do know that we can't just lie down and take it. There has to be a way that you can still have the life you want. You heard what Dr. Harlow said...."

Ian scowled at her. "Screw what Dr. Harlow said."

Jordan pressed her lips together to stop herself from challenging Ian. He needed her support, not a lecture.

He shook his head as he looked down at the floor. After a couple tense, silent seconds, he said, "I won't be able to give you children."

Jordan felt her stomach lurch, and tears born of sadness and loss welled up in her eyes. She quickly pinched her eyes and forced the tears back.

"Did you hear me?" Ian snapped the question at her.

"Yes," Jordan said calmly. "I heard you."

"And you mean to tell me—" he looked over at her "—that you're *fine* with never having a family? That you're really going to tie yourself down with a man who won't give you a baby?"

Before she could answer him, he stood up and began to pace. "The thing is, I really feel like I've been deluding myself this whole time about our relationship. I'd actually *convinced* myself that you would be fine with not having what most women want…."

Jordan sat stock-still on the couch. She felt she was on trial by fire without having committed a crime. Everything was happening too fast—coming *at her* too fast. Of course she had considered the idea of having children with Ian; it was a natural thing for a woman who wanted children to do. But was Ian's decision not to have biological children a deal breaker for her? It was unexpected, yes. It was sad. But it didn't change the fact that Ian was the man she wanted to spend the rest of her life with. She wanted to marry this man. She wanted to be his wife. And there was always adoption.

"What I'm saying—" Ian sat down heavily in a chair that was half the room away from her "—is that I love you enough to let you go, Jordan. You deserve to be with someone who can give you everything you want, including children of your own."

"But…I'm not asking to be let go, Ian." She crossed her arms protectively in front of her stomach. "And unless you're breaking up with me right now… I mean, is that what you're doing? Trying to let me down gently?"

"No," he said. "I'm trying to be fair to you."

"Then I'm not going anywhere," Jordan stated with quiet conviction.

"Are you saying that you want to marry a man who—" Ian started to count his fingers "—isn't going to have a career, a driver's license, *independence*…?"

"I don't believe that's what's going to happen." Jordan shook her head.

His features hardened. "Then maybe you're just as delusional as I am, Jordan. I've researched Stargardt, too. There are *a lot* of people, *young* people, with this disease who are on disability because they can't hold down a job. That's reality. That's the truth."

"And I've seen people online who have *great* lives... challenging, yes, but still great! I've seen painters on those websites...equestrians, mountain climbers—*photographers!*"

When Ian dropped his head back into his hands and refused to answer her, Jordan crossed the room to him. She sat down cross-legged on the floor and grabbed his hands. She could feel the residue of freshly shed tears on his fingertips. She pressed her forehead to their clasped hands.

"Don't shut me out of your life, Ian. Don't shut me out," she said with a catch in her voice. "I love you so much. And I think that maybe—just maybe—God put me through all those really tough times with Grandpa so...I could be prepared...when I met you."

She waited for her words to sink into Ian's heart, and when they finally did, he untangled his hands from her grip, wrapped his arms around her and held on to her tightly. He bunched the material of her shirt in his fists as he pulled her closer still.

"We'll get through this together, Ian," Jordan said softly into his ear. "Don't shut me out. Okay? Promise me."

After a few moments, he pulled back so he could kiss her. She placed her hands on either side of his face and kissed him back deeply—trying, through her kiss, to reassure him of her devotion and love.

"Promise me," she said against Ian's lips.

"I promise," Ian said, then sat back and wiped his eyes with the sleeve of his shirt.

Jordan put her hands on his knees. "It's been a long, tough day."

"Long. Tough. Inevitable," he said wearily. "I'm sorry that I took it out on you. None of this is your fault...."

Jordan grasped his knees and moved them back and

forth. "You don't need to apologize to me, Ian. I understand. I really do. I'm just glad that you let me be here for you today."

He took her hand in his and guided her up so they were both standing. Then he hugged her tightly, and she knew he meant the hug to be a thank-you and an apology all wrapped up in one.

Jordan turned her head so her cheek was over Ian's heart. "This is totally off topic, so I apologize, but…are you as hungry as I am?"

He rested his chin on her head. "I could eat."

"Italian?" Jordan leaned back so she could look up into his face.

"Whatever you want."

"Old Spaghetti Factory? Garlic Mizithra for two?"

Ian lifted her chin with his fingers and kissed her lightly. "That's fine. I'd just like to get some work done before we eat, okay?"

Jordan could read him like a book: he needed to find a way to feel a sense of normalcy again, and he could do that by throwing himself back into work.

"Me, too." She gave him one last squeeze before she stepped out of his arms.

There were too many empty canvases in her makeshift studio waiting to be filled up with paint. Day by day, her gallery deadline was looming closer, and she still had so much work to do.

"I'll order, and when the food arrives, I'll meet you back here."

Ian gave her a faint smile before he disappeared behind the room divider. Jordan took her cell phone out of her pocket and discovered that the battery was dead. Not having her charger at the studio, she ordered their food from Ian's landline and then headed upstairs to her studio. She had just started to pour paint out onto her palette when she heard a loud knock at the door.

Surprised, she checked her watch. "That's a new record."

She twisted the lid back on to the tube of paint and headed back downstairs. Jordan had a friendly smile on her face as she opened the door, but the smile quickly faded when she saw who was standing on the other side.

Chapter Thirteen

"Surprise!" A loud chorus of voices greeted her as she opened the door.

Jordan stood speechless and motionless as she stared at her family. Her dad, mom, eldest brother, sister-in-law and Josephine were squeezed tightly together in the entrance of the studio, shoulder to shoulder, and beaming at her as if they had just given her the greatest gift in the world. The only one *not* beaming was her sister, who looked as if she had just been kidnapped by a gang of wild bandits.

"Why don't you have your phone on?" Jo asked with an irritated shake of her head. "I've been *trying* to get hold of you."

"My battery's dead," Jordan said as she stared dumbly at her family.

"Oh! It's better this way." Barbara Brand reached out for her youngest daughter, cupped her face in her soft hands and smiled brightly at her. "Jordan loves surprises!"

"I do?" Jordan asked as she gave her mom a hug.

As was her norm, Barbara Brand wore her platinum hair slicked back into a chignon, her makeup was subtle and flawlessly applied and she smelled faintly of Coco Mademoiselle. She had remained Chicago chic even after four decades of living on a Montana cattle ranch.

"Of course you do!" Barbara exclaimed as she entered Ian's studio and spun around to take in the architectural features of the space. "Or is that Jo who loves surprises?"

"That's me," Jo said as she hugged her sister tightly, then whispered, "Sorry. I tried to warn you."

Still too stunned to formulate a rational question, Jordan found herself being embraced by her sister-in-law, Sophia.

"Jordy!" Sophia said as she squeezed her tightly while swaying slightly to the left and then to the right. "I'm so glad to see you! I love your hair!"

Lovely Sophia, with her easy smile, bright hazel-green eyes and flowing honey-blond hair was as sweet as a Krispy Kreme doughnut and just as difficult to resist.

"I'm happy to see you, too," Jordan said halfheartedly. She didn't want to hurt Sophia's feelings, but just couldn't muster the same amount of enthusiasm for this surprise family reunion.

"I like this color much better." Barbara agreed with Sophia. "It's a very chic cut."

"I thought you were going to be in Boston this week…?" Jordan asked her parents as she looked over her shoulder to see if Ian had come to investigate. The last thing he needed, after the day he just had, was to have his studio overrun by her boisterous family.

"We were. But Luke and Sophia needed to come to San Diego, so we thought we'd tag along and make an event of it," Barbara said as she put her purse on Ian's conference table and looked around the studio. "This is a *gorgeous* old building. I really love that they left the old exposed brick when they renovated."

"Good to see you, Jordan," her eldest brother said as he walked through the door.

"Hi, Luke," Jordan replied, before she greeted her father.

"How's my daughter?" Her dad smiled down at her affectionately.

Henry "Hank" Brand was tall and lean, with a shock of gray hair that was usually covered, as it was now, with a Stetson cowboy hat. He wore his "dressy" dark jeans with a large, polished-silver belt buckle from his rodeo days. With his sun-weathered skin and his intense blue eyes, he looked as if he'd stepped right out of a John Wayne Western.

Jordan gave her father a quick hug before she shut the door. "I'm good, Dad."

She was surprised that Ian hadn't appeared yet, but knew that it was only a matter of time before her two worlds—California and Montana—would collide.

"He needs to be changed." Luke was holding her squirming, fussing two-year-old nephew, Daniel. "Where's the closest bathroom?"

"Oh, I'll take care of it." Sophia held out her arms to her chubby, tow-headed son; she took Danny and the diaper bag from Luke. "You stay and catch up with your sister." Then she looked down at her son affectionately and asked, "Can you say 'hello' to your auntie Jordan?"

"Hi, Danny." Jordan reached out and touched his soft hand. "You were a wrinkly little raisin the last time I saw you."

Danny, who looked back at her with those bright blue Brand eyes, turned beet red in the face and started to scream when she touched him.

Jordan withdrew her hand and looked up at Luke with raised eyebrows. "Well—his lungs work."

"I'm so sorry." Sophia sent her an apologetic smile. "It's been a really long day for him, poor guy. Bathroom?"

Jordan pointed in the direction of Ian's custom-designed Italian-marble bathroom and cringed at the thought of it being used as a diaper-changing depot. Horrible thought.

"Okay, I'm confused," Jordan said as she looked at her family, who had gathered near Ian's conference table. "*Why* are you all here in San Diego?"

"I'm EOSing." Luke said in his quiet, controlled voice.

Luke wasn't as tall as their father, but he was broad shouldered and made from lean muscle. A captain in the United States Marine Corps, he wore his military bearing as a badge of honor. Even out of uniform, as he was now, there was no mistaking his ramrod-straight back and wide-legged stance.

"EOSing?" Jordan asked.

"End of service." Luke stood with his arms behind his back, looking like an oddity in Ian's industrial, modern loft. "I'm retiring."

"Well, that's good news," Jordan said to her brother. The last thing her parents needed was to bury another son.

"Your mom thought it'd fun to get the whole family involved." Hank took off his hat and set it on the table. "You know how she gets."

"But how did you know I was here?" Jordan glanced over at Jo.

"Don't look at me." Her sister held up her hands defensively.

"We stopped by the condo first." Barbara smiled. "It's so *tiny,* Jordan. I wish you'd think about moving into a place that isn't so *cramped.*"

"It's fine, Mom," she said with a sigh.

"Anyway, Amaya gave us the address. She says that you spend most of your time here anyway." Barbara pulled out one of the chairs and sat down.

"Don't be mad at her, Jordy," Jo said as she leaned against the back of the sofa. "It was a matter of survival."

"I don't know what you're talking about," Barbara said defensively.

"Yes, you do," Jo said to their mom, then turned to Jordan. "She started to rearrange your living room in order to increase feng shui...."

"There's nothing wrong with a little feng shui," Barbara insisted as she looked at the family. "Right?"

"And that would have been fine, sort of, if you hadn't started to badger poor Amaya about everything from her makeup to her hair to her education...her *career*...her *sex life. Contraception.*"

"Uh...*wow!*" Jordan exclaimed. "Mom. Really?"

"What?" Barbara asked, genuinely confused by her daughters' reaction. "Her entire family lives a world away in another country. I was just trying to give her some much-needed motherly advice. What's wrong with that?"

"*Unsolicited* advice." Jo looked over at her with raised brows. "Now do you see why you shouldn't be mad at Amaya?"

"And why should she be mad anyway?" their mom asked no one in particular. "I didn't realize this was a secret. Why is it a secret?"

"It's not," Jordan said. "I told you that Ian was letting me work in his studio. But I wouldn't have agreed to host an impromptu family reunion here. This isn't my place."

"We've been trying to call you all day to let you know that we were flying in," Barbara said. "But you can't expect us to not even try to see you while we're here...."

Before Jordan could reply, she saw Ian appear from the back of the studio. She immediately walked over to him.

"I'm sorry," she said under her breath as she moved to his right side.

"It's fine," Ian assured her softly.

She glanced up at his perfectly chiseled face and was shocked to discover that there wasn't even an ounce of tension around his mouth or jaw. Ian was taking this Brand family invasion in stride. She wished she could do the same; she felt like a nervous wreck inside and couldn't quite pinpoint why.

"Ian, this is my family. Family, this is Ian." She felt the color drain from her face as drops of sweat rolled down to her rib cage from her suddenly damp armpits.

"Ian Sterling." He smiled as he held out his hand to her father. Ian always extended his hand first to camouflage his difficulty with depth perception.

"A pleasure, sir." Hank gave his hand a quick, hardy shake. "Sorry to barge in on you like this."

"Not at all…." Ian said.

"It's been a long time since I've seen my youngest," Hank explained.

"I understand," he said sincerely. "If I were in your shoes, I would've tracked her down, too."

Josephine stepped forward and gave Ian a quick hug hello, while Jordan tried to be mindful of his vision deficits as she began to introduce her clan one by one. He had just finished shaking Luke's hand and thanking him for his service when Sophia emerged from the bathroom carrying a subdued Danny, who was happily drinking from a sippy cup.

"Hi!" Sophia greeted Ian with her trademark smile.

"Hello." He smiled back at her, then reached out slowly to ruffle Danny's fine blond hair, while Jordan held her breath and hoped he didn't overreach. Danny stared at him with his wide blue eyes, but didn't immediately melt down as he had with her.

"I'm so sorry," Sophia said in a loud whisper to Jordan. "I looked high and low for an air freshener. It's a little pungent in there."

Jordan cringed and wished that her family wasn't always so "open" about things.

"Don't worry. I'll take care of it," she said to Sophia before she addressed Ian. "Ian, I'd like you to meet my sister-in-law, Sophia, and my nephew, Danny. Sophia, this is Ian Sterling."

Sophia's grabbed his hand and shook it. She had a slightly starstruck expression on her pretty face. "I'm such a *huge* fan of your work. My husband—" she nodded toward Luke "—made me leave my copy of your book at home because he thought it'd be rude for me to ask you for an autograph right off the bat...."

"Not at all," Ian said again.

"I think your work in black-and-white is truly remarkable." Sophia continued to hold on to his hand.

"Thank you," he said graciously.

"I'm an unrequited photographer," Sophia explained as she finally let go of Ian's hand. "I'd really love to see some of the photographs you've taken of Jordan."

"So would I," Barbara said, positioning herself closer to him. "Anyone who could finally get Jordan in front of a camera is a person after my own heart. I've been trying to get both of my girls to model for years and years...."

"I just showed Jordan how beautifully she could photograph. That's all I did." Ian put his arm around her shoulders. "I'd be happy to show you some of her work."

Jordan had been vague about her relationship with Ian. She had told her parents that they were dating casually, but

Ian's body language as he stood next to her wasn't even remotely vague. He was making an unspoken declaration that they were "together," and she only hoped that her mom wouldn't turn this into an interrogation. Today of all days, Ian didn't need that kind of hassle.

"And I want to see these new paintings I've been hearing about while we're here, Jordan," her dad interjected.

Jordan grimaced as she shrugged one shoulder. "There really isn't all that much to see. I still have a lot of work to do before my February 1 deadline."

Ian immediately jumped to her defense; he knew that both of her parents were upset by her decision to drop out of graduate school.

"Sometimes the creative process takes time. But what she's been working on is impressive. She has a modern, unique style, and I'm really proud of what she's accomplished in a short amount of time."

"Thank you," Jordan said softly as he pulled her more snugly into his body.

Ian offered everyone something to drink and then took them to the computer to show them her images. She hung back and watched him interact with her family. She couldn't have predicted it, but Ian fit right into her family as if he was the last puzzle piece that completed the picture. He was relaxed around her father and Luke, and she could tell he had managed to charm her mother pretty quickly. Barbara was smiling at him, genuinely laughing at his comments, and she had touched his arm affectionately several times.

"He's doing a lot better than Brice did," Jo whispered next to her. "I'll give him that."

"I know—right?" Jordan said under her breath. "I've never seen anyone win Mom over that quickly. This has gotta be a new record."

"Gotta be," Jo agreed.

Once the family had viewed the photographs Ian had taken of her, the entire gang headed up to her studio to take a look at the paintings she had been preparing for the gallery show. While they were crammed into her small space, there was a knock on the door.

"Food's here," Jordan said to Ian.

"I'll get it," he answered. "You stay here."

"We were hoping we'd be able to talk y'all into joining us for dinner," Hank said.

Jordan looked over at Ian. She knew he tried to avoid situations that made it difficult for him to compensate for his vision deficits.

"I don't know, Dad." She tried to beg off quickly. "Ian has a lot of work to do tonight. And we already ordered food."

"I'll just put it in the refrigerator for later," Ian surprised her by saying. "We'd love to join you."

"Are you sure?" The question popped out of her mouth. They'd had an emotional day, and although he hadn't freaked out over her family showing up at his studio unannounced, she just couldn't image that he would deliberately *prolong* it. "I mean—" Jordan tried to soften the question as her family looked at her curiously "—you have so much work to do."

"Nothing that can't wait," Ian said, before he headed down the stairs to answer the door.

After losing both his parents, he knew the importance of spending time with family. And knowing that Jordan was the woman he wanted to marry, he had only one chance to make a great first impression.

With Ian's vision in mind, Jordan suggested one of his favorite haunts for the family dinner. Jordan's mom insisted on sitting next to Ian, and the two of them talked nonstop throughout the entire meal. Barbara Brand was an avid traveler and they spent the majority of the evening comparing notes of their favorite travel destinations.

When it was apparent that Ian was holding his own with her family, Jordan was able to relax and enjoy seeing her parents and her siblings. One hour blended into the next as they ordered, finished their main courses and then indulged in dessert. Afterward, Sophia pulled up a chair in between Jo and Jordan.

"We're going to have to get Danny back to the hotel." Sophia glanced over at her son, who was sleeping in Luke's arms. "But I wanted to show you guys something before we go."

The sisters leaned in as Sophia scrolled through some pictures on her phone. She found the one she wanted, selected it and then enlarged it.

They looked at the sonogram displayed on Sophia's phone for several seconds before it hit Jordan. "Oh, my God, Soph—are you pregnant?"

"You're pregnant?" Jo asked excitedly. "How far along are you?"

"Just a little over three months," she said with a broad smile. "But do you notice anything unusual?"

Jordan shook her head, confused, but then Jo said, "Wait a minute—are there *two* arrows?"

"Ho-ly crap, Soph! You're having twins?" Jordan asked.

"It was bound to happen, right?" Sophia asked with a laugh.

"Nice work, Luke." Jordan gave Luke a thumbs-up across the table. "He didn't waste any time, did he?"

"No. He didn't," Sophia said, as the skin on her neck and cheeks turned a pretty shade of pink.

"Congratulations, Sophia." Jo gave her sister-in-law a hug.

"Yeah. Congrats, Soph." Jordan made it a triple hug.

Soon after Sophia shared her news, Ian insisted on picking up the check, and then everyone slowly made their way to the door.

Barbara Brand linked her arm with Jordan's. "We're going to stop by your cousin's new bakery tomorrow. I think it'd be nice if you'd come with us and show Mackenzie your support. She's had a tough time these past couple years. You know her daughter, Hope, has been so sick."

"Okay." Jordan nodded. "I've been meaning to get in touch with her."

Barbara leaned in closer. "I like him," she said of Ian. "He's a gentleman, just like your father...and so *handsome*."

"I'm glad the two of you hit it off, Mom," Jordan said.

Their family was tight-knit and it had always been important for her parents to approve of the man she wanted to marry.

"And I already invited him to the ranch, so you make sure he comes out for a visit," Barbara said.

"You invited him to Montana?" Jordan asked, shocked.

"Honey—" Barbara stopped just outside the restaurant door and hugged Jordan tightly "—if he's important to you, then he's important to me. And I promise I'll stop trying to get you to move back home. You have a life here. I can see that. But you can't blame me for missing you."

"I always miss you, too, Mom," Jordan said as she kissed her on the cheek.

It took a while for everyone to say goodbye, but once Danny started to have a meltdown, they wrapped up the visit and went their separate ways. And by the time Jordan and Ian returned to the loft, neither one of them felt like working.

They sat down on the couch and Ian put his arm around

Jordan's shoulders. She snuggled into the side of his body and sighed.

"How are you doing? We've had a crazy day...."

"I'm okay. My eyes are tired, but I'm okay," Ian said as he closed his eyes to rest them.

"Well...I'm exhausted," she said with a yawn. "I love them, but they wear me out. I wish they didn't always have to travel in a pack!"

"You have a great family." Ian ran his fingers through her hair. "Your mom's a hoot."

"That's one way of putting it." Jordan smiled. "Why am I not surprised that you charmed her in five seconds flat? She actually invited you to the ranch!"

"Yeah—how 'bout that?" Ian chuckled. "Do you think the rest of your family liked me?"

Jordan leaned back so she could look up at him. "Yeah, I do. My dad called you 'buddy.' He only does that with people he likes."

"Luke's a hard one to read." Ian rubbed his hand over her arm.

"He changed a lot after he joined the U.S. Marines. Tyler, my middle brother, is super chill. You'll meet him when you visit the ranch." Jordan pushed herself up so she could look more directly into Ian's face. "You know, I'm really sorry that they just barged in the way they did. You'd already had a pretty crappy day and then my whole family shows up unannounced...."

"Don't worry about it, Jordan," Ian said as he pulled her back against his side. "I'd rather meet the in-laws sooner than later."

"Your in-laws?" Jordan shifted in his arms. "Is that what you just called them?"

Ian turned his head toward her and cracked open his

eyes. "One day I'm going to marry you, Jordan. Any objection to that?"

"No." She draped her leg over his and put her hand on his stomach as she pressed herself more firmly into his body. "No objection at all, GQ."

Jordan's schedule during the month following her family's visit was balls-to-the-walls busy, and it felt as if she hadn't had enough to time to catch her breath, much less find time to paint. Ian was working like a man possessed, pushing up photo shoots whenever possible and working late into the night. Because he was so pressed for time, Jordan had taken it upon herself to manage his vision-related appointments, including hunting down a low-vision equipment specialist who could offer technology solutions in both the penthouse and the studio. Ian's new eyeglass prescription was filled and he was also fitted for special protective contact lenses. She had also consulted with a dietician and made contact with the support groups.

Jordan was proud of everything she had done to help Ian maintain his independence. But with all the time and energy she put into modeling or helping him, she often felt too drained to paint. Her gallery show was three short months away and she was genuinely concerned that she wouldn't be able to make her deadline. Not only did she feel stressed out about her lack of progress on her paintings, but she was troubled by her relationship with Ian. Over the past couple weeks, the tension between them had been building. They didn't fight, they didn't even really disagree and yet it felt as if they had both retreated to their own proverbial corners of a boxing ring, and at any time they could come out swinging.

Alone in her studio, Jordan stared at the empty canvas in front of her. She had been looking at it, uninspired and frustrated, for nearly an hour. Now that they had finished shooting for the book, she was finally able to focus entirely on her art. But she soon realized that her desire, her *drive,* to paint had fizzled. She felt exhausted and emotionally drained, and her eroding relationship with Ian was weighing heavily on her mind. There were many nights when he slept on the couch when he returned to the penthouse rather than joining her in his own bed. And there were some nights when he didn't bother to return to the penthouse at all. Instead, he would sleep at the studio, and would already be working at his computer by the time she arrived with breakfast. And although Ian denied that there was anything "wrong," and assured her that things between them would get better once he finished working on the book, Jordan wasn't convinced. Their lovemaking had tapered off and there was a chronic feeling of indifference between them that was becoming impossible for Jordan to ignore.

After an hour of racking her brain about her next painting, she gave up on inspiration and headed downstairs to find Ian. As was usual, he was sitting in front of his computer, sifting through the hundreds of images he had taken for the book. He had his new reading glasses on and was using the Zoom Text software that had been installed on his computer, allowing him to enlarge the images to a size he was able to see.

"Hi," she said as she walked over to where he was working.

"Hi." He barely glanced her way when he greeted her. Ian refused to let anything divert him from his work on the book, and Jordan envied his ability to compartmentalize his life.

"Take a look at this shot," he said excitedly as he pulled

up one of the last photographs he had taken of her on the final shoot on the USS *Midway* Museum.

Jordan moved a step closer so she could get a better look at the image. She saw herself lying on her back on top of a Cougar, a vintage navy airplane known for flying photograph reconnaissance missions in the 1950s. Her back was arched to follow the curve of the cockpit of the plane, and her face was turned to the camera.

Ian zoomed in on her face. "Look at the expression in your eyes. I think this is the best photograph I've ever taken of you."

Jordan saw the haunted, sad look there and was immediately transported back to that day. She hadn't been acting—she had been genuinely sad. The night before that photo shoot, she had brought up adoption as a way for them to have a family together, and Ian had told her, in no uncertain terms, that he had no intention of adopting. He had given her an ultimatum: if she wanted to be his wife, she would have to accept the fact that she would never be a mother. It had taken a while for that conversation to sink in fully, but now that it had, Jordan found it difficult to think about anything else.

She put her palm on his shoulder as she stared at her own image. Ian reached over and gave her hand a placating, platonic pat before he grabbed the mouse again. Stung, Jordan removed her hand from his shoulder and tucked it into her pocket.

"How's it going up there?" he asked, seemingly oblivious that she was upset.

"Not so good." She sounded fatigued and exasperated, and wondered if Ian noticed anything about her anymore.

Perhaps it was seeing herself in the photograph looking so depressed and morose, or perhaps it was the dismissive pat that Ian had given her hand, but something in her snapped, like the minuscule straw that finally broke the camel's back.

"Ian," Jordan said wearily. "We have to talk."

Chapter Fourteen

For the first time that day, Ian really looked at her. He swiveled his chair toward her and squinted up at her face through his reading glasses.

"You sound upset," he noted cautiously. "What's wrong?"

"I am upset," Jordan said. "And I really think that we need to…clear the air."

Ian's brows drew together in concern as he nodded. "Okay."

He followed her over to the U-shaped couch and sat down in his usual spot. She sat across from him on the other side of the couch. It struck her as ironic that they were seated exactly as they had been the day of her first test shoot. It seemed to her that they had come full circle without even realizing it.

"What's up?" he asked her. He wasn't relaxed back in the couch as he normally would be. Instead, he was sitting upright, and she could tell by the tension around his mouth and jawline that he was bracing himself for something unpleasant.

"This isn't working for me," Jordan said, more bluntly than she had intended.

Ian's expression changed from concerned to confused. "What are you talking about?"

She crossed her arms and leaned forward. Her nerves were making her stomach churn, and it was actually starting to hurt.

"I'm talking about us, our relationship." Jordan hugged her arms more tightly around her body. "Things haven't been right between us for a while now and I just can't stand it anymore."

Ian stared to the right of her shoulder, and she understood that he was looking around his blind spot so he could see her more clearly. It didn't appear that he was looking at her, but she knew he was.

After a moment of peering at her, perplexed, as if she had just grown a third head, he rubbed his hands over his face in a familiar sign of frustration.

"Jesus, Jordan," he said, exasperated. "You know I've been working like a dog to get through these photo shoots. I never misled you about *any* of this. You knew I wouldn't have much downtime to spend with you, but I promised that I'd make it up to you once I got the book squared away. We've already talked about this. Why do we have to rehash this thing over and over again?"

"I know you've been busy," she replied in a measured, tense voice. "But being busy and being checked out from this relationship are two entirely different things."

"Checked out?" Ian asked. "I'm not checked out, Jordan. I'm *focused,* on my *work,* which is what you should be—focused on painting."

"You can believe me or not, Ian. But the truth is the truth, and we've become…*roommates.* Half the time you don't even sleep in bed with me…." She was hurt and it resonated in her voice.

"Because I don't want to disturb you. Jesus! Why am I being *crucified* for being *considerate?*"

"Ian. You can stick your head in the sand and ignore the writing on the wall, but I can't."

"What writing on what wall?" His expression had turned stony.

Jordan felt as if she had been chewing on cotton balls. Her mouth was dry and her words were jammed up in her throat. She knew what she needed to say, but it hurt her to say it. She loved Ian. That hadn't changed, and she couldn't imagine a time in her life when it would change.

"Wait a minute," he said, with a ripple of anxiety creeping into the baritone timbre of his voice. "Are you breaking up with me?"

"Ian…you know things haven't been right with us…." Jordan said quietly. "Something's been bothering you for a while now and whenever I ask you what's wrong, you give me the same answers again and again—I'm tired, I'm working, *nothing*…."

He stood up and strode over to the wet bar. He uncorked the Scotch and reached for a glass. Crystal clinked as he overreached and pushed the glasses together. Ian cursed under his breath as he reached a second time for a tumbler.

"I *say* that I'm tired and I'm working because I *am* tired and I *am* working!"

"It's more than that," she said, as he poured himself a Scotch neat. "You shouldn't be drinking that," she added when he brought the tumbler to his lips.

Ian tipped his head back, downed the Scotch and then slammed the glass on the counter. He turned toward her.

"That," he said angrily. "That right there is a big part of the problem."

"At least you're finally admitting that there *is* a problem," Jordan said caustically. She knew her tone would spark his temper, but she couldn't bring herself to regulate it. This was the first sign of emotion she had gotten from him in a while, and his anger would be a vast improvement over his indifference.

"You're smothering me," Ian said tersely as he sat down heavily on the couch. "You micromanage *everything*—my diet, when I should go to the doctor…my *drinking*. I want to be your man, Jordan, not your pet project."

"I was just trying to help," she said, stunned. "I had no idea you felt this way."

"I didn't want to hurt your feelings, Jordan." Ian tried to soften the blow. "I knew you were trying your best to help me, and I do appreciate everything you've done for me…."

"You have a funny way of showing it," she muttered under her breath.

"But…" Ian ignored her comment as he continued, "It's just too much. I've never wanted you to stop painting in order to take care of me. You know that's true…."

"I do," Jordan agreed. He bugged her about painting all the time.

"Look, Jordan…." He softened his tone. "I understand that part of you has been trying to make up for all of the things you weren't able to do for your grandfather…."

When Ian mentioned her grandpa, Jordan felt the tears she had been forcing down try to push their way to the surface.

"I get that. And I can appreciate it. I really do…." Ian said gently. "But I can't stand the idea that you're using helping me as an excuse not to succeed."

She swiped at the tears that had slipped out of her eyes. "What do you mean by *that?*"

"I mean—" Ian leaned forward and rested his forearms on his thighs "—that you've been spending too much time managing *my* life when you should've been managing your own. Every time I ask you about the show, you tell me that you'd start working on the new paintings once we were done shooting the book. We're done shooting for the book, Jordan, and you're *still* not painting. And the only reason I can come up with is that you're afraid to succeed."

"I'm not afraid to succeed!" she snapped at him. "That's *not* the reason I haven't been painting."

"Then what is it?" he asked. "Because I've been really worried about you, Jordan.... I feel like you're going to miss your deadline, and I know this gallery owner. If you don't deliver when she's put her ass on the line for you, you may as well just dump your brushes in the trash along with your reputation."

"I know," Jordan said under her breath. She knew Ian was right; he was only putting spoken words to her own private thoughts.

"So...what's going on with you, Jordan? If you tell me, maybe I can help *you* for a change."

She stood up, walked over to one of the tall windows and looked down at the activity on the street below. She turned her back to the windows and leaned against the sill.

She didn't want to say what she was about to say. She was going to hurt both of them—there was no way around it.

"Can you come away from the window? I can't see you."

Jordan returned to the couch and perched on the edge. She crossed her arms protectively in front of her body and then said, "I haven't been able to paint because I've been upset about what's going on with us...."

Ian took several seconds to process that information before he responded. He sounded genuinely concerned when he said, "That can't be true."

"It is true," Jordan said. "I can't *block* everything out the way you can and just keep on working. If something's bothering me, it impacts everything about me, including my painting."

He dropped his head into his hands as he thought. When he lifted it again, he said, "Now I understand why you didn't want us to get involved. If you're distracted, you can't work."

She nodded imperceptibly. "Yes."

"I would never want our relationship to stand in your way, Jordan," Ian said. "From my perspective, I didn't think things were all that bad between us. But, okay... now that I *do* know, what can I do to help you get back on track so you can meet your deadline?"

Jordan hesitated before she answered. "I think I need to find another place to paint."

He sat forward. "Wait a minute.... Did you just say that you think you need to find another place to paint? As in you want to move out of here?"

"I think that's what's best for me," Jordan said, as she swallowed back the acid that had raced up her throat.

The muscles in Ian's jaw worked. "Now, look, Jordan—you wanted to get my attention, so you've got it. Okay? I get that you want more of my time, and I'll work on that—I give you my word. You don't have to move out to make a point."

"I wasn't trying to make a point," she said. "I'm trying to tell you what I need to do so I can meet my deadline."

"You think that getting away from me is going to help you paint?" Ian asked accusingly. "Jesus, Jordan...how long have you been thinking about this?"

"For a while…." It wasn't cold in the loft, but she felt chilled all over her body.

"And you didn't bother to bring it up until now?" he asked incredulously.

"I wanted to wait until we were done shooting for the book," she explained.

"This isn't the kind of thing you hold back, Jordan! This is the kind of thing that you bring up before we get past the point of no return!" Ian's face had turned ashen beneath his tan. "Is that what you're saying here? That we're past the point of no return? Because when someone starts to talk about moving out, that's just code for breaking up. I asked you once before—*are you* breaking up with me? Is that what this is?"

"Yes." Her voice cracked on the answer.

The room became very still, as if the oxygen had been sucked right out of the space.

Ian was so still for so long that Jordan jumped when he suddenly stood up and marched back over to the wet bar to pour himself another drink. With his back toward her, he swallowed the liquid down. He splayed his hands out on the marble and leaned against his arms, head lowered.

"There has to be more to this," he said under his breath. "This doesn't make sense." He turned around. "Are you involved with someone else?"

"You know better than that."

"Then what?" He sliced his hand through the air. "What is *so terrible* about our relationship, Jordan?"

"I didn't say that our relationship was terrible…."

"You're right." Ian raised his voice. "Because you haven't really said anything at all except you can't paint around me! Tell me something that makes sense here, Jordan. I may be going blind, but I can hear just fine! Why are you walking out on me?"

"Because we don't want the same things out of life, Ian."

"What are you *talking* about?"

"Children." Jordan said the word, but it came out muddled. She cleared her throat and repeated, "Children."

He shook his head slowly in disbelief. "Dammit...not *this* again. We already *settled* this!"

"Just because you decided the subject was closed, Ian, doesn't mean that it was settled." Jordan stood up and walked over to the kitchen island and positioned herself to his right side. "It wasn't settled—not for me."

"You knew—" Ian punched one hand into the other "—that I wasn't going to have children. If it was such a big problem for you, you should've walked away a long time ago! Why drag us through all of this if you knew you were just going to leave in the end?"

"I accept the fact that you don't want to have biological children, Ian. I do. But you want me to accept that if I marry you I'll never be a mom...that I'll never have a family. And I can't accept that. I've wanted to be a mom for as long as I can remember. Like painting...like loving you... being a mom is something I feel like I was *born* to do."

"You'd rather be a mom than my wife...." Ian said bitterly.

Jordan crossed her arms tightly over her chest. "I don't see why I have to choose. There are so many children who need a good home. Nothing is stopping us from adopting."

"I've already told you, Jordan...." Ian bit out the words. "I'm not going to saddle some poor kid with a blind father. I'm not going to take on the responsibility of another human being when I can't even guarantee that I'll be able to take care of myself! Why can't you *understand* that?"

"I do understand," Jordan said sadly. "I just don't agree with it."

Ian's body language mirrored hers, with his arms

crossed protectively in front of him. "I'm not going to change my mind about this, Jordan."

More tears slipped onto her cheeks. "I know, Ian. Neither am I."

His eyes were glassy with emotion. "So...that's it? You're leaving me...."

Jordan fumbled with her keys as she pulled them out of her pocket. She had to leave now. She couldn't look at Ian for one more second; she wouldn't be able to stop herself from reaching out to him if she didn't leave now.

Ian, who had been standing stock-still, jumped into action when he heard her keys rattle together. He followed her to the door. "Where are you going?"

"Home." She wanted her bed. Her pillows. Her comforter. Hibernation was the only reasonable next step for her.

"Why?" he asked.

Jordan paused at the door, heard the exhaustion in her voice as she said, "I have a lot to do, Ian. I need to find a new place to paint, like, yesterday. And if it's okay with you, I'll get my stuff out of the penthouse tomorrow while you're here."

"Jordan." He reached out for her hand and missed. "Wait a minute. What the hell just happened here? I don't want us to break up. I love you."

She slipped her fingers into his searching hand. "I love you, too, Ian. But that doesn't mean we should spend the rest of our lives together. It's better for both of us that we figured this out now, because when push comes to shove, Ian, we just don't want the same things."

She turned the knob to open the door and tried to slip her hand out of his. But Ian tightened his grip on her fingers and pulled her into his arms. Jordan didn't resist. As his lips covered hers, as his strong arms encircled her body, she kissed him with all the desperation and sadness of a woman who was saying goodbye to the man she loved. Ian's body was shaking as his strong arms held her tightly against him. After several poignant last minutes in his arms, she stepped away from him. She opened the door and walked into the reception area.

"This isn't what I wanted…." Ian said from the open doorway.

"I know." Jordan pressed her forehead on the exterior door as her hand gripped the doorknob. "Neither did I."

"When will I see you again?" His voice was strained.

"You won't," she said as her brain ordered her fingers to turn the knob. "It would just be too…painful. For both of us. We need to give each other a chance to move on."

Ian stood frozen in the doorway, stunned, as if someone had just punched him in the gut. He strained to focus in on Jordan as she paused in the open doorway.

"Take care of yourself, Ian," she said as she forced herself to turn the knob, walk through the door and out of his life.

"Don't go, Jordan," Ian said, but then he realized he was talking to himself. She was already gone.

"I can't believe you're moving out, Jordy. Why can't you just ignore Ian's ginormous building that you can see from every conceivable angle of our condo, and just *stay?*"

Jordan finished taping up her last box before she walked over and gave her roommate a hug. "I can't do it anymore, Amaya. It's just…too much."

"I know." Amaya's shoulders slumped. "I wish *he* would move. Jerk!"

"He's not a jerk, Amaya. It just didn't work out between us, that's all," Jordan said as she looked up at Ian's building. "And in a way I have him to thank for my show. If he hadn't pulled some strings to get me that loft space down the street, I don't know how I would've met the deadline."

"You have *yourself* to thank," her friend said sourly. "You're way too forgiving, Jordy. I don't want to talk about him anymore. Talking about him is a major buzz kill."

Jordan knew that there was no sense defending Ian. Amaya was her friend and staunchly loyal, and all she knew was that Ian had broken her heart. And he had. Even though she had been the one to break things off, Jordan still loved him. And from the very beginning of their breakup Ian had reached out to her. He had emailed and texted and called. But he never said anything new. He never said anything different. He had called her for Thanksgiving and Christmas, but when he didn't contact her for New Year's, Jordan finally gave up hope that he would change his mind about having a family.

"So what are you going to wear to Altitude tonight for the big Valentine's bash?" Jordan asked to change the subject.

Amaya's face brightened as she opened the sliding glass door and lit a cigarette. "I found the cutest, raciest little dress! Wait till you get a load of it. I'm so glad that you're coming. You've been like a hermit, all cooped up in here. It's been *super* depressing to watch."

"Gee, thanks." Jordan smiled as she labeled the last box with an indelible marker.

"Don't you flake out on me, Jordy!" Amaya pointed her cigarette at her. "I swear I'll find someone to make out with you tonight. And if I *don't,* I'll plant a big wet one on you myself!"

"You don't have to go that far." Jordan laughed. Her phone rang and she pulled it out of her pocket.

"Hey, Matthew. What's up?" she asked as she walked into the kitchen. She put her hand on the refrigerator handle, but paused while she listened to one of the representatives at the gallery. "Oh. Well…that's good news. Okay. Thanks for letting me know."

Jordan slipped the phone back into her pocket, got a glass of water and then sat down at the dining table.

"What's wrong with you?" Amaya asked as she stubbed out her cigarette. "You look nauseous."

"Another one of my paintings just sold at the gallery."

Her friend stepped inside and closed the sliding glass door. "That's great news, right?"

"Sure."

Amaya joined her at the table. After sitting down, she put her foot up on the chair and rested her arm on her bent knee. "So then why don't you *look* like it's good news?"

Jordan shrugged. "It was one of my favorites."

Curaçao Sunrise, the painting that had just sold, was the only one she had painted of Ian. The piece depicted him running on the beach with the sun rising behind him, and she had vacillated for weeks before she had decided to put a price tag on it and include it in the show. And now that it had been sold, she regretted her decision.

Amaya stared at her suspiciously. "No! Don't you start moping again, Jordy! I forbid it! Come on." She dropped her foot to the floor and bounced out of her chair. "Let's get ready. I feel like getting drunk and dancing until I pass out."

"Do you always have to be such an extremist, Amaya?" Jordan shook her head at her friend.

"Yes, I do," she replied as she went down the spiral staircase. "And shave your legs and pits! You never know, you might just get laid tonight."

"*Zero* chance of that," Jordan said under her breath as she walked into the kitchen.

She had put her empty glass in the sink and was heading toward the stairs when she heard the doorbell ring. She could hear that Amaya was in the shower.

"I'll get it!" she called out.

Jordan peeked through the peephole and saw a man in a brown uniform holding a giant bouquet of long-stemmed roses. Surprised, she opened the door.

"Ms. Jordan Brand?"

"That's me."

"I have a delivery for you, ma'am." The man held out his electronic pad for her to sign.

Jordan quickly scrawled her name and then accepted the heavy flower arrangement. "Thank you," she said, before she smelled the fragrance of one of the roses closest to her nose.

"Have a nice day."

Jordan shut the door and carried the bouquet to her room. She set them on her nightstand and then excitedly looked for a card. She spun the leaded crystal vase around and discovered that there was a sunflower, her favorite flower, tucked in front of the roses. Attached to it was a small envelope. Jordan touched the sunflower lightly before she detached the envelope and pulled out the card inside. She sat down on the bed and read the message.

Beautiful Jordan,
The roses are for Valentine's Day. The sunflower is
so you know that I was listening....
Love always,
Ian

"Who are those from?" Amaya stood in the doorway, wrapped in a towel and dripping water onto the carpet.

"Ian," Jordan said, as she reread the card for the fourth time.

"Well, I'll say this for him. He certainly knows how to kiss up successfully." Amaya walked over to the flowers and smelled them. "What are you going to do about it?"

"I have no idea," she said pensively. "I think there may be too much water under that bridge."

Chapter Fifteen

Ian walked into the living room wearing his best black tuxedo. "How do I look?"

"Good." Dylan nodded.

"Is my bow tie straight?" Ian fidgeted nervously with his tie.

"It's fine," Dylan assured him. "Relax. Everything's going to work out. When she gets those flowers, she's gonna call."

"I hope you're right." Ian smoothed his hands over his jacket. "I don't want to get stuck with you as my Valentine."

"I think she'll call," his friend said. "I'd rather not be your runner-up."

"Did the painting arrive?"

"Yep." Dylan relaxed back into his chair. "They delivered it while you were getting ready, and I had them hang it in the entryway. It's framed, it's done, downlighting and all. Jordan will see it the minute she walks through the door."

"If..." Ian tugged on the cuffs of his crisp white shirt once more. *"If* she walks through the door."

"She'll come," Dylan said again. "Do you have the ring?"

Ian pulled a small black box out of his pocket. "Right here."

After watching him pace around the penthouse like a caged tiger, Dylan said, "Will you sit down, man? You're making *me* nervous."

Ian sank down in one of the living room chairs and tapped his foot nervously on the marble floor. He had planned a very special Valentine's date for Jordan, but knew that all his careful plans could be for naught. It was a long shot, a Hail Mary pass, to imagine that she would actually accept his unconventional invitation. But before he could extend that invitation, she needed to receive the flowers, and then take the step to call or text to say thank-you. If she received the flowers and didn't contact him, then he would know, without any doubt, that she was lost to him forever.

"Did you check on the chef? Is everything set in the kitchen?" Ian asked. He was having his private chef cook all Jordan's favorite foods.

"It's all good."

"What about the table on the terrace? Did you see candles? I definitely want there to be candles."

"Ian—everything's perfect. Jordan's going to be blown away, swept off her feet, I promise you." Dylan looked at the time on his phone. "After tonight, you and she are going to be copacetic."

Just as Ian was about to answer, his phone whistled to signal that an email had just arrived. He dug the device out of his pocket and brought it close to his face. He strained to read the message.

"Dammit! Look at this, Dylan, and tell me if it's from the florist."

Dylan looked at the email. "The flowers were delivered."

"All right." Ian held out his hand for his phone. "Now we wait."

Dylan silently prayed for Jordan to pick up the phone and call his friend. He knew just how much Ian had riding on this plan panning out. And Dylan, almost as much as Ian, wanted this to work. It had been really tough to watch his best friend lose his eyesight *and* the love of his life at the same time. He had helped Ian plan and execute this surprise Valentine's date, but ultimately, it was all in Jordan's hands. And Dylan prayed that she still loved Ian enough to give him one more chance to make things right between them.

"It's been a while now, right?" Ian asked.

"No. It's been, like, five minutes. Give her a minute to work through it. Remember, those flowers came out of left field."

"You're right." Ian nodded as he wiped his sweaty palms on his pants.

Inside his head, Ian was pleading with Jordan to pick up the phone and call. He had missed her in a way he hadn't even known was humanly possible. Missing Jordan had been a chronic soreness in his muscles and an ache in his bones. He had lost a friend, his closest ally, when he had lost her, and he was determined to do whatever he had to do to get her back. He just hoped that it wasn't too little too late. But when thirty minutes passed after he'd received the delivery notification, he started to lose hope.

Maybe she didn't love him anymore. Maybe she was already involved with someone else. Maybe—

"Ian!" Dylan's loud voice interrupted his pessimistic ruminations.

"What?"

"Your phone's ringing!"

"Dammit." He fished for his phone, which had fallen between his leg and the chair arm. It rang three times before he was finally able to retrieve it and push the button to answer.

"Hello?" He hadn't been able to see the name attached to the incoming call. "Hello?" It could be Jordan or it could be someone else.

"Ian?" He heard the sweet sound of her voice and dropped his head back, smiled broadly and punched the air above his head with his fist.

"Jordan," he said, as Dylan clasped his hand in a brotherly, congratulatory handshake. "It's really good to hear your voice."

There was a pause on the other end of the line before she said, "It's good to hear your voice, too, Ian."

Not really knowing what else to say, he asked, "How are you?"

"I'm okay," she said quietly. "How are you?"

"I miss you," Ian said honestly. He couldn't hold anything back, not now. Not tonight.

"I got the flowers, Ian. They're beautiful." There was a raw, vulnerable quality in Jordan's voice that struck a chord in his heart, gave him hope. Jordan still cared for him.

"I'm glad you like them." He tried to steady the quaver in his voice. He was so nervous and excited to be talking to her that his heart was beating wildly in his chest.

"I do," Jordan said softly. "I do like them. But…why did you send them?"

"Because I was hoping that you would want to give me a call to thank me."

"Thank you," she said, and this time he actually heard a smile in her voice. She had called and he had made her smile—that was half the battle won right there. But he didn't want to get cocky. Jordan always had to be handled with care. When he forgot that, he lost her. If he won her back, he wouldn't ever make that mistake again.

After a lull in the conversation, Jordan started to say, "Well…I'd better—"

"Jordan." Ian interrupted her so she wouldn't get off the phone. "It's Valentine's Day, as you know, and I'd like to ask you out…on a date."

She didn't answer, so Ian started to talk fast. "I know I'm springing all of this on you and that you might already have plans, but if you're free, or if you have plans that you can change, I would be very honored if you would join me tonight at the penthouse for dinner."

He jiggled his knee up and down rapidly and rested his forehead in his hand while he waited for her to give him her answer. There were several long, excruciating seconds of silence before she said, "I do have plans tonight."

Ian's stomach bunched up in a knot as he prayed that she wasn't going to turn him down.

"But—" Jordan said after another pause "—they aren't set in stone."

He jumped out of his chair. "That's a yes, right? Thank you, Jordan. I promise you won't regret it. I'll have David pick you up in an hour. Is an hour okay or do you need more time to get ready?"

"An hour's fine…but, Ian. Wait. I do want to come over. I do want to see you again. But…"

"Jordan," he said in a rush, "I'm sorry I interrupted you, but I already know what you were going to say. You want to know if anything's changed. And without going into too much detail on the phone, let me just say this—for me, everything has changed. I promise you, Jordan. I'm not wasting your time." Ian closed his eyes. "Jordan. Please. Just come over. Give me a chance to make things right between us."

"Okay, Ian," she said gently. "I'll see you in an hour."

After she hung up the phone, he looked in the direction where he knew Dylan was sitting. Incredulous, Ian exclaimed, "I'll be damned! She actually said yes!"

It was only a short distance to his condo, but Ian had sent the Bentley to pick her up. As she slid into the backseat and moved her hands over the supple leather seats, she could feel Ian's energy in the car. She could smell a faint hint of that spicy, delectable cologne that always drove her senses mad. Her entire body was trembling with anticipation and trepidation as David pulled in front of Harbor Club Towers. He parked and then came around to her door. He offered her his hand and she accepted.

"May I say," David said as he closed the door, "it's good to see you again, Ms. Brand."

"Thank you, David," she said sincerely. "It's good to see you, too."

"And may I also say—" he tipped his hat to her "—you look lovely tonight."

Jordan glanced down at the midnight-blue cocktail dress that her mother had insisted she buy, but she had never worn until tonight. "I hope I'm not overdressed."

"No. You got it just right," the chauffeur assured her. "Mr. Sterling has a very special evening planned for you." David walked with her to the front door of the building and opened it for her. "Enjoy your evening, Ms. Brand."

Jordan rode the elevator up forty floors. She felt jittery

and freaked out, and didn't know what she was doing back in Ian's building. She had thought it was over between them, and now, out of the blue, he was back in her life. Was she crazy to be here?

As she stepped out of the elevator, she felt a little bit as if she was returning to the scene of a crime. Instead of heading directly to Ian's condo, she walked in small circles in front of the closed elevator doors, holding her arms out from her sides so the AC would cool her perspiring armpits.

"You either do this or you don't." She stopped in place and scolded herself. "What's it going to be? Make up your mind. One way or the other."

After her moment of self-talk, she tossed up her hands and headed toward Ian's door. There was a doorman waiting to open it for her, who no doubt had seen her acting crazy in front of the elevator and had tagged her as a nut job.

The minute Jordan stepped into Ian's ornate foyer, she saw her painting, *Curaçao Sunrise,* hanging on the wall, with downlighting.

"Oh, my God," she said under her breath as she walked slowly over to it. She reached out and ran her hand lovingly over the frame. To the painting that she loved and had thought she had lost, she said, "There you are."

Jordan was touched by Ian's simple, quiet gesture of love and support. And it bolstered her hope that taking a chance, seeing him again, was a gamble that was going to pay off…for the both of them.

With a renewed sense of confidence, she climbed the marble stairs and up into Ian's world. Poised at the top of the steps, she eagerly searched the great room for her first glimpse of the man she still desperately loved. There, standing by the wall of windows, dapper in his black tuxedo, with the dusky San Diego sky as a backdrop, Ian was waiting for her. She hadn't said a word, but he turned around and faced her.

"Jordan?" he asked. "Is that you?"

And there it was—that swarm of butterflies fluttering in her stomach the moment she heard the sensual sound of his voice as he said her name.

"Yes." Jordan took a step toward him. "I'm here."

She crossed the room to where he was standing, then stopped a few feet away from him and let her greedy eyes roam his handsome face. How she had missed this man. But when she sought out Ian's eyes, it struck her instantly that he wasn't making eye contact with her. While she was away from him, while they were apart, his ability to do so had been lost. He was looking in her direction, but he wasn't looking into her eyes.

"How are you?" Jordan asked, wanting to reach out to him.

Ian's hands were tucked away in his pockets. "Do you want the polite answer or do you want the truth?"

"The truth."

"I'm 20/200 in both eyes now, Jordan," he said quietly. "I'm legally blind."

His words, words that weren't completely unexpected, broke her heart.

"Oh...." Jordan said without thought as she dug her fingers into her arm.

Ian took a step toward her—he wanted to comfort her. "But I'm okay, Jordan."

She lifted her hand to her throat. "You're okay?"

"Actually, I am." He took another step toward her. "And I don't want us to dwell on that tonight. Not tonight."

"Okay, Ian." Jordan knew that although he couldn't see the pain in her eyes, he could hear the pain in her voice.

Ian's personal chef appeared from the kitchen, shattering the tension. "Dinner is served, Mr. Sterling."

"Thank you," Ian said as he held out his arm to her. "Shall we?"

Jordan accepted his arm, and touching Ian again felt as if she was coming home. She felt the bulge of his biceps beneath the fine material of his tuxedo jacket, and she breathed in that familiar, masculine scent that was so wonderfully Ian.

"We'll be dining on your favorite balcony tonight." He covered her hand with his. "If you don't mind steering us through the doorway…. I hate to admit it, but I sometimes need more than one try to get through a doorway unscathed."

Jordan glanced up at him in surprise. She had never heard him joke about his condition. It seemed that Ian's eyes had gotten worse, but his attitude had improved.

"Oh, Ian." She paused just beyond the French doors. "It's beautiful."

A table set for two, with crystal and fine linens and candles, was placed to maximize her favorite view of the San Diego harbor.

"You did this all for me?" she asked, as he pulled out her chair for her. She was always aware that he was relying on his peripheral vision to help him navigate his world, and she helped him whenever she could without being too obvious.

Ian joined her at the table. "I was trying to make an impression."

"Well, you *did* that." Jordan looked out at the harbor before she turned her head back to him. "You must've been pretty certain I'd come."

"No. Not certain," Ian said. "Hopeful. I was *hopeful* you'd come."

A waiter arrived with a bottle; he quietly poured them each a glass.

"I took the liberty of ordering sparkling cider for two." Ian slid his hand across the tablecloth until his fingers made contact with the base of his wineglass. "I'm taking a break from the hard stuff."

"That works for me," Jordan said as she lifted up her glass. "What shall we toast to?"

"To the success of your show," he said as he held up his glass to her. "I'm so proud of you, Jordan."

"Thank you." She took a sip of her sparkling cider, and then it hit her—she hadn't even mentioned the painting in the foyer. "Ian… I can't believe I didn't mention this the minute I saw you. I suppose I was too…overwhelmed by seeing you again…. You bought *Curaçao Sunrise!*"

"I wanted to have part of you with me, no matter what happened between us tonight," he said with a pleased smile. "Besides…I wasn't about to let someone else own a painting that I thought was always meant for me."

"It was meant for you," Jordan said. "It was always meant for you. And I feel really…honored that you bought it."

"The honor is mine, beautiful." Ian used her lover's nickname for the first time and it made her stomach flip-flop. "Happy Valentine's Day."

Jordan touched her glass to his one more time. "Happy Valentine's Day."

One by one, the waiter delivered all her favorite dishes: hearts-of-palm salad, lobster bisque, salmon fillet with baby asparagus. And for dessert, chocolate-marble cheese-cake. During the meal, the conversation was easy and comfortable, as if they had never been apart. Ian wanted to hear about her family and about the success of her show. And he filled her in about the progress of the book that had brought them together in the first place. They talked about many things as they enjoyed their meal, but Jordan knew that Ian was building to something. Something he would share when the time was right.

"Okay...." She groaned as she put her hands on her stomach. "I'm stuffed and I'm cold."

Ian had given her his jacket halfway through the meal, but even with the added warmth, the chill in the air was too brisk to be comfortable.

"Let's get you inside," he said. "We can have coffee in my study...in front of the fire."

"Perfect." Jordan took hold of his arm and helped guide him back inside.

Once settled in his study with mugs of coffee and a lit fire, Ian dismissed the staff, and then they were finally alone for the first time in months.

"That was an amazing meal, Ian. Thank you," Jordan said as she slipped out of his jacket.

"You're welcome." He sat down next to her. "I wanted to make sure, if you *did* accept my invitation, that you would feel how much...I still love you. How much I've missed you."

She reached out and put her hand on his. "I do feel loved, Ian. And...I want you to know that I love you, too. Very much."

He intertwined his fingers with hers. "You know...my life fell apart the day I lost you. But I didn't know it right away. I had the book to keep my mind busy. Once that job was done, that's when it really hit me just how much I had lost the day I let you walk out the door."

Ian paused before continuing. "You know...I didn't think anything could be worse than losing my eyesight." He shook his head slightly. "But nothing prepared me for what it was going to feel like to lose you. And I knew that if I was ever going to have a chance of winning you back, I was going to have to change. But change isn't easy. It takes time. And I didn't even know where to begin, didn't even really believe that I could change enough to…make things work between us. But I just missed you so damn much, Jordan, that I felt like I had to try…."

She held on tightly to his hand. "What did you do?"

"I went back to my shrink, for one. Then I went to a support-group meeting," he said with a smile in her direction. "And I know what you're thinking. You can't believe that I actually went to one of those things—but that should prove to you just how much I wanted you back."

"I'm shocked," Jordan said. "I admit it. I never thought, not in a million years, that you would actually agree to go to one of those meetings. You were just so…*adamant* about not going."

"You're right. I was…. But go I did."

"And…?"

"And I met a lot of really impressive people, Jordan. For the first time, I met people like me, who had Stargardt… who understood *exactly* what I was going through. I'd always thought that support groups were for weak-minded whiners, but…I was wrong. I've made a lot of friends and they have careers, they have…families. And even though it's challenging for them, and none of them deny that or try to sugarcoat it, they're *succeeding.* And meeting them, hearing about their successes, made it seem somehow possible for me. It made me think that maybe Dylan's idea for us to start a modeling agency isn't so far-fetched after all. And it made me think that maybe the idea of…you and me wasn't so far-fetched, either."

"Are you saying that…you're willing to have a family, Ian?"

"I don't know if my…diagnosis…would stop us from

being able to adopt, Jordan. But I've always wanted a family. And I'm not going to let Stargardt stop me from having a family with you. I'm willing to give adoption a try."

"Are you sure, Ian?" Her voice trembled on the question.

"I've never been more sure about anything in my life, Jordan." Ian wished that he could see her lovely face more clearly. "Jordan…can I touch your face?"

She lifted his hand so he could feel the contours of her face. His fingertips gently touched her forehead, her cheeks, her lips….

"Why are you crying?" he asked, concerned.

"They're happy tears." Jordan pressed his hand to her face. "Because I love you so much, Ian. I've missed you so much."

"Beautiful…" He gathered her into the safe harbor of his arms. "Come here. Let me hold you."

Jordan placed her palm on his heart, felt it beating strong and fast. She tucked her face into his neck and breathed in his scent. "You smell so good," she murmured.

Ian tilted up her chin and brushed his fingers lightly over her mouth before he brought his lips to hers. He kissed her gently, tentatively…tenderly. Jordan was the one to deepen the kiss, to deepen the connection between them. Ian's lips took a sensual path down the side of her neck, and she sighed at the feel of his mouth on her skin.

"You taste good," he whispered into her ear. "I've missed you so much, you have no idea."

He started to untangle himself from their embrace, and Jordan stretched out her hand. "Where are you going?"

"Not far." He smiled in her direction. "There's something I need to do, and I've been waiting impatiently all night to do it."

He got down on one knee beside the couch and held his hand out, palm up. "May I have your hand, Ms. Brand?"

Jordan gave it to him. "What are you doing?"

"I'm doing what I should have done a long time ago," Ian said. He reached into his pocket and pulled out a small, velvet box.

Jordan's eyes widened as she watched him flip open the lid with his thumb. He held the box up for her to see the contents.

She gave an audible gasp when she saw the ring inside. "Oh, my God, Ian," she said, and her hand went up to her throat. "It's the blue diamond."

Inside the box was the two-carat, cushion-cut blue diamond that she had worn during the Elite Jewelry photo shoot.

"The minute I saw this ring on your finger, I knew it was meant to be yours," Ian said.

Jordan swiped fresh tears from her cheeks, but couldn't find any words to respond. This night—this incredible, surprising, romantic night—was a dream…a dream that she hoped she would never awaken from.

"Jordan…" Ian said. "You're the woman I've been looking for all my life, and I never want to be apart from you again."

He let go of her hand so he could take the ring out of the box. With the aid of his peripheral vision, and Jordan's help, he took her left hand in his. He poised the sparkling blue diamond at the tip of her ring finger as he continued.

"Will you marry me, Jordan? Will you be my wife?"

"Yes." She laughed through her happy tears. "Yes, Ian. Of course I'll marry you!"

With a shaking hand, he slipped the diamond over her knuckle until it was seated firmly on her ring finger.

"You're trembling," Jordan said as she pulled him up to join her on the couch.

Ian gripped her hand in his. "I'm nervous."

She placed her palm on his cheek. "You don't ever need to be nervous with me, Ian. I love you with all of my heart."

He scooped her up and set her in his lap. Jordan wrapped her arms around his shoulders and kissed him passionately.

"Jordan," Ian said against her mouth. "You're going to be my wife."

She tilted her head back and laughed. "I know. My silly high school fantasy actually came true."

"A story to tell our children," he said as his lips explored her neck.

"And our grandchildren." Jordan gasped as Ian's teeth grazed her earlobe.

She shuddered as every cell in her body revved up for the lovemaking that was only moments away. She could hardly wait to have Ian fill her as he joined his body with hers.

"And our great-grandchildren," he said seductively, slowly beginning to unzip her dress.

"Ian…" Jordan said on a breath as his large, warm hand slipped inside.

"Yes, Mrs. Sterling?" he asked, smoothly unhooking her bra.

"I want to get married in Montana…with my whole family there," she told him as he started to slip her dress slowly off her shoulders.

"Whatever you want, my beautiful bride…." Jordan arched her back when he pressed his lips to the swell of her breast.

"And Ian…?" She ran her fingers over his shorn hair.

"Yes, my love?" Ian asked with a frustrated laugh.

Jordan put her hands on either side of his face to make certain he was paying attention to her.

"Promise me that we'll always stay together. No mat-

ter how much I annoy you or irritate you or micromanage you...."

"I promise." He flashed one of his famous, charming
smiles that showed off his dimple.

"I'm going to hold you to that, GQ." Jordan tugged the
knot on his bow tie loose.

"Beautiful..." Ian said as he brought his lips to hers. "I
wouldn't want it any other way."

* * * * *

COMING NEXT MONTH FROM

HARLEQUIN®

SPECIAL EDITION

Available March 20, 2014

#2323 A HOUSE FULL OF FORTUNES!
The Fortunes of Texas: Welcome to Horseback Hollow
by Judy Duarte
Toby Fortune Jones knows his purpose in life. He's a cowboy and foster dad to three adorable kids. But Angie Edwards is still drifting—until she meets Toby. Suddenly, Angie gets swept up into a life she's always dreamed of...but is she ready, willing and able to make a family with the fetching Fortune?

#2324 MORE THAN SHE EXPECTED
Jersey Boys • by Karen Templeton
Tyler Noble's happily-ever-after involves nothing more than his salvage business and his rescue dog. When pregnant beauty Laurel Kent moves in next door, however, troubled Tyler finds his outlook on life slowly changing. Can "Mr. Right Now" leave his past behind to create a forever family with Laurel?

#2325 A CAMDEN FAMILY WEDDING
The Camdens of Colorado • by Victoria Pade
Dane Camden is only interested in working on his grandmother's happily-ever-after...until he meets Vonni Hunter. Eager to settle down—but not with bachelor Dane—Vonni's hesitant about taking a job planning the Camden matriarch's nuptials. But she can't deny her attraction to the hunky Camden as she realizes domestic bliss might just be closer than she thinks.

#2326 ONE NIGHT WITH THE BOSS
The Bachelors of Blackwater Lake • by Teresa Southwick
Olivia Lawson wants her boss, Brady O'Keefe, more than any raise. Brady's seemingly oblivious to her feelings, so Olivia decides to move away and start a new life. When the boss demands a reason for her departure, Olivia invents a fake boyfriend. But Brady's not buying her fib—or the sudden turn of events that might take his gorgeous assistant away forever....

#2327 CELEBRATION'S BABY
Celebrations, Inc. • by Nancy Robards Thompson
When a one-night affair leaves journalist Bia Anderson pregnant, her best friend, Aiden Woods, steps up as her child's "father"—and her fiancé. Little does Bia know, though, that Aiden's been in love with her for years, but has never acted on it. As they bond over her unborn baby, a friendship turns into the love of a lifetime.

#2328 RECIPE FOR ROMANCE • by Olivia Miles
Baker Emily Porter is shocked when her long-lost love, Scott Collins, comes back to town. Scott's got an unwelcome secret—and it's not just that he's still madly in love with Emily. Tension rises as sparks fly between the ex-lovers, but will long-buried lies destroy their relationship?

YOU CAN FIND MORE INFORMATION ON UPCOMING HARLEQUIN® TITLES, FREE EXCERPTS AND MORE AT WWW.HARLEQUIN.COM.

HSECNM0314

***

"If you didn't meet him on vacation, it must have been a trip for work," said Brady.

"Remind me not to try and put anything over on you."

Sarcasm was one of his favorite things about her. "So, was it in Austin? Seattle? Atlanta?"

"I definitely went to those cities. You should know. We were there together."

She was right about that, but when business hours were over they'd gone their separate ways. If Olivia had met men, she'd never said anything to him. Until now.

As crazy as he knew it was, he wanted to know everything. "Do you have a job lined up in Leonard's neck of the woods?"

"I have an offer."

"I'd be happy to give you a glowing recommendation."

She stood and walked to the doorway of his office. "Any other questions?"

Why are you leaving me?

Brady didn't say that out loud, even though the idea of it

had preoccupied him way too much since she'd dropped her bombshell. Besides his mother, sister and niece, he had no personal attachments—yet somehow he'd become attached to Olivia. He wouldn't be making that mistake with his next assistant.

She looked over her shoulder on the way out the door. "I'll be lining up more candidates to interview. And if you know what's good for you, you'll approach this process more seriously than you just did."

"I conducted those interviews very seriously."

She ignored that. "You need to ask yourself what's wrong with the two women you saw today."

"I don't need to ask myself anything. I already know what's wrong."

"Care to share?" She put a hand on her hip.

"Neither of them is you."

***

Enjoy this sneak peek from Teresa Southwick's
ONE NIGHT WITH THE BOSS,
the latest installment in her
Harlequin® Special Edition miniseries
THE BACHELORS OF BLACKWATER LAKE,
on sale in April 2014!

◆ HARLEQUIN®

SPECIAL EDITION

Life, Love and Family

Coming next month from
USA TODAY bestselling author
Victoria Pade

A CAMDEN FAMILY WEDDING

Dane Camden's only interested in working on his
grandmother's happily-ever-after…until he meets
Vonni Hunter. Eager to settle down—but not with
bachelor Dane—Vonni's hesitant about taking a job
planning the Camden matriarch's nuptials. But she
can't deny her attraction to the hunky Camden as
she realizes domestic bliss might just be closer than
she thinks.

Look for the latest in
THE CAMDENS OF COLORADO *miniseries*
next month from Harlequin® Special Edition®
wherever books and ebooks are sold!

HSE65807